"Don't you bel
I could make

Pippa swallowed, left speechless by his unexpected question. At last she found her voice. "Love can't be forced."

"No?" Carlos said. "But perhaps it can be cajoled."

Before she knew what he was about, Carlos's lips claimed hers in a kiss that was insistently intimate. At first she resisted. Then, as he pressed kiss after kiss on her trembling mouth, Pippa began kissing him back with unbelievable yearning.

At last he released her, and a bemused Pippa stared up at him, color flooding her cheeks.

Then, when she saw the arrogant satisfaction in his dark eyes, fury replaced desire.

10644503

ANNABEL MURRAY has pursued many hobbies. She helped found an arts group in Liverpool, England, where she lives with her husband and two daughters. She loves drama: she appeared in many stage productions and went on to write an award-winning historical play. She uses all her experiences—holidays being no exception—to flesh out her characters' backgrounds and create believable settings for her romance novels.

Books by Annabel Murray

HARLEQUIN PRESENTS
933—LAND OF THUNDER
972—FANTASY WOMAN
1029—NO STRINGS ATTACHED
1076—GIFT BEYOND PRICE

HARLEQUIN ROMANCE
2596—THE CHRYSANTHEMUM AND THE SWORD
2612—VILLA OF VENGEANCE
2625—DEAR GREEN ISLE
2717—THE COTSWOLD LION
2782—THE PLUMED SERPENT
2819—WILD FOR TO HOLD
2843—RING OF CLADDAGH
2932—HEART'S TREASURE
2952—COLOUR THE SKY RED

Don't miss any of our special offers. Write to us at the following address for information on our newest releases.

Harlequin Reader Service
901 Fuhrmann Blvd., P.O. Box 1397, Buffalo, NY 14240
Canadian address: P.O. Box 603,
Fort Erie, Ont. L2A 5X3

ANNABEL MURRAY

a promise kept

Harlequin Books

TORONTO • NEW YORK • LONDON
AMSTERDAM • PARIS • SYDNEY • HAMBURG
STOCKHOLM • ATHENS • TOKYO • MILAN

Harlequin Presents first edition February 1989
ISBN 0-373-11148-7

Original hardcover edition published in 1987
by Mills & Boon Limited

Copyright © 1987 by Annabel Murray. All rights reserved.
Cover illustration copyright © 1989 by Tony Meers.
Except for use in any review, the reproduction or utilization
of this work in whole or in part in any form by any electronic,
mechanical or other means, now known or hereafter invented,
including xerography, photocopying and recording,
or in any information storage or retrieval system, is forbidden without
the permission of the publisher, Harlequin Enterprises Limited,
225 Duncan Mill Road, Don Mills, Ontario, Canada M3B 3K9.

All the characters in this book have no existence outside the
imagination of the author and have no relation whatsoever to
anyone bearing the same name or names. They are not even
distantly inspired by any individual known or unknown to the
author, and all incidents are pure invention.

® are Trademarks registered in the United States Patent and
Trademark Office and in other countries.

Printed in U.S.A.

CHAPTER ONE

'PIPPA, I can't stop you seeing this man—if you choose to do so, but I confess, I'd rather you *didn't* receive him.'

James Lang threw the letter and the envelope with its foreign stamp and postmark on to his desk.

Pippa gave her father a long considering look, her fine grey eyes, which could be disconcertingly shrewd, studying his troubled face. She supposed, loving James as she did, that his words alone should be sufficient deterrent. But then, the lean, scholarly man who confronted her had never imposed his will on her. Throughout her childhood—and this had been a bone of contention between him and her mother—he had always led, cajoled, but never driven his daughter to obedience.

Besides, if Pippa had one besetting sin it was curiosity, and she was curious now, feeling that the answers to questions many years unresolved were within her grasp.

'He says he's coming with a message from my mother.' Pippa picked up the discarded letter and studied the bold black writing. The writer's English, though stilted and formal, was impeccably correct. The signature—Carlos de Alvarez—was large, forcibly written, nearly scoring through the paper.

'That's precisely why I'd rather you didn't see him. Your mother chose to walk out of this house thirteen years ago. In all that time I've heard from her only once—and through the mouth of the same intermediary.' James's fine, sensitive lips tightened, as though the thought of the man whose letter Pippa still held was distasteful to him. 'And I'd prefer that *you* didn't have any communication with her at all.'

'But if Senhor de Alvarez has come specially all the way from Portugal,' Pippa urged, 'surely the least we can do is to hear what he has to say? And he does say here,' she consulted the letter once more, 'that he is particularly anxious to talk to *me*.'

'I don't want you to have anything to do with your mother *or* her family,' James persisted. Inez Lang had been a de Alvarez before her marriage. His thin face was flushed with angry blood. By nature James was a placid man, but he *could* be roused to anger, though this was a rare occurrence these days. But Pippa could remember a time—a time before her mother had left home—when the house had been rent by the sounds of their constant quarrels.

Pippa was not afraid of James's rare anger. She knew it was not directed at her. He'd been really angry with her only once—six years ago—when she'd been not quite sixteen—and that had been her own stupid fault. She'd fully deserved his censure. Father and daughter, in fact, shared a deep affection, and until recently Pippa had always supposed that once—despite their rows— Inez must have loved him too.

She felt a deep pity for her father and indignation against her mother, but in spite of this, curiosity won the day.

'I'm sorry, Dad, but I think I'd better see him,' she decided, 'or I'll always be wondering ...'

'Damn it, Pippa!' James complained. 'I did think I could expect some loyalty from you after all these years, and in the circumstances. Your mother has Mariana— she was always more her daughter than mine anyway— but I've always thought of you as *my* daughter.'

Pippa had to acknowledge that she resembled her father rather than the de Alvarez side of the family. She had his height, his red-gold hair, but her fiery temperament was not his, but her mother's.

'I *am* your daughter,' she reassured him, 'but I'm also my mother's. Nothing can change that.' It was an affirmation, not defiance.

Pippa often wondered what her life would have been like now, if she had been the younger daughter, and accompanied her mother back to Portugal, instead of being left in England. Because Inez *had* left her behind, Pippa had always felt her mother could not have loved her as well as she did the younger Mariana, whom she could only remember as being a dark-haired, solemn four-year-old. But she knew now that Inez had not willingly left her behind.

'Very well!' James said suddenly, interrupting her train of thought. 'See the man. As you're constantly reminding me these days, you're an adult now. But if de Alvarez wants to see you, he must do so in my presence.'

'But I thought you didn't want to . . .?'

'I still don't. But as you're so determined . . . And God knows what lies he might try to tell you. Besides,' grimly, 'I must admit to a certain curiosity. Why should the de Alvarez family want to get in touch with us again, after all these years?'

James Lang could not be more curious than his daughter to hear what Carlos de Alvarez had to say, Pippa thought. But lies? Whose were the lies? Until recently, she had believed implicitly what her father had told her—that her mother had had no cause for dissatisfaction with her marriage. But now she knew better—knew of Inez's restlessness, her unhappiness.

One thing she could be sure of, it couldn't have been

James's fault Inez had left. He was no bully, though in one sense he had always been a domestic tyrant. Vague, introspective, impractical, he expected family life to revolve around him. Pippa had wondered sometimes recently if that was why he'd married Inez, product of an upbringing that demanded a woman's dedication to the needs of her father, brothers and husband. But Inez had proved to be untypical of her kind and in the end she had rebelled.

It was only a few weeks ago, looking through a trunkful of possessions, obviously swept away into a corner of the attic after her mother's departure, that Pippa had found the complete disproof of her father's claims, her mother's diaries, written partly in English, partly—her secret thoughts perhaps—in Portuguese, which Pippa did not understand.

According to the diaries, Inez had married an Englishman—in the first instance in defiance of her father's wishes that she marry the man of *his* choice—in the second place because of her belief that the wives of Englishmen were more emancipated. Too late, she'd discovered that all this particular Englishman wanted was an efficient capable wife, devoted to domesticity and his comfort, and who could provide the children he desired. Pippa was well aware that, much as he loved her, James had been disappointed that neither she nor Mariana had been a boy.

Hesitantly, because she feared to reopen old wounds, Pippa had asked her father about the diaries, but he had showed less concern than she'd expected.

'Those old things—I didn't realise we still had then.'

'Have you—have you ever read them?'

'Lord, no—they were just Inez's scribblings.'

'Not even to find out why—why she went away?'

'Your mother went away,' James said wryly, 'because—so she said—she could no longer endure the cat-and-dog life we led. I suppose you don't remember the scenes?'

'Oh yes, I remember ... But Dad, I've always wondered, why did she take Mariana—and not me?'

'Because,' fiercely, 'I wouldn't let her. I told her, "Take Mariana if you must. She's still a baby. But you're not going to uproot Pippa, take her away, from everything she knows—her friends, her school, her home." Do you blame me? Would you rather have been brought up in Portugal?'

'No, of course not,' she reassured him with real affection in her face and voice. 'I've been perfectly happy living here, with you.'

But to a certain extent, Pippa could sympathise with her mother. No man, she vowed, was ever going to take away her independence, the opportunity of a career. Over the years she had quietly nurtured her talent, a compelling way with words; and she was certain that, given the opportunity, she had it in her to become a fine writer.

One puzzle remained. Why, after a marriage enduring ten years, had Inez suddenly left her husband? The diary—the last in a series—which had divulged the facts, had stopped several weeks short of Inez's departure for Portugal.

'But don't let this de Alvarez fellow get under your skin,' James Lang warned his daughter now. 'He's an arrogant beggar. All the de Alvarezes were arrogant. I've only met this one twice—six years ago—and long before that, when he was a toffee-nosed little brat of thirteen. I doubt he's changed much.'

* * *

Deus, how interminably boring were these narrow, winding country lanes, how incredibly dense those of whom he enquired his way! Carlos de Alvarez was not in the best of humours as he manoeuvred the hired car through the already wintry Suffolk countryside. He had little relish for his present errand, but he had given his word.

He would be glad when his mission was accomplished and he could return to the sunshine of his home. How did they endure, these English, to live in such a damp, bone-chilling climate? Even in the coldest months of the year, Sintra was never like this.

How remote from civilisation had Inez's existence been, how different from the Portuguese way of life. The wonder was that she had endured it even for ten years.

At last! Little Pennyfeather! Ridiculous name! Unlike the names of the towns and villages of Portugal, it seemed to have no meaning. Over the river bridge—how vividly he remembered that river—past the little grey church, through the farmyard and beyond to the 'big house'.

Now he was in the village, he remembered the route. He had traversed it once before to no purpose, and he hoped this second journey would not turn out to be as fruitless as the first—though as to its outcome ... His shoulders, in the expensively tailored, well-fitting suit, rose in a shrug of resignation. What would be would be. He had given his word, but if the fates conspired against him? It was of little moment to him, though, apparently, of great consequence to Inez, and even a de Alvarez could not direct the hand of fate.

To the accompaniment of barking dogs—how English houses smelled of insanitarily damp animals!—the front door was opened—not by a servant as would be the case at the Quinta, his own country house, but by the owner himself, James Lang. Six years had not made much alteration to Inez's husband, Carlos thought. The Englishman was a little greyer perhaps, a little more stooped, but his eye was as fierce, his mouth as thinly disapproving as on the last occasion they'd met.

And yet, as a young man, Carlos remembered, the Englishman had been diffident and shy. No doubt his years with Inez had wrought the change. She was not, he'd had cause to discover himself, an easy woman to live with.

Carlos surveyed James with mixed emotions. Was he to be denied access to Inez's elder daughter yet again? They had agreed, Inez and he, that now the girl was in her twenties her father could scarcely prevent the interview—unless, of course, the girl herself was unwilling?

Just what had her father told her about the de Alvarez family? What had she thought, or been taught to think, about her mother's defection?

'Senhor Lang! Carlos de Alvarez—you recall?'

'Your name and your face are not things I'm likely to forget,' the Englishman retorted sarcastically. 'You'd better come in. I'll call Pippa. She's somewhere around the place. She should have been at work, but since you've decided to "honour" us with a visit . . .'

Carlos shivered again, as he was shown into a large drawing-room, comfortably, but shabbily furnished. These English—were they ashamed of wealth that they made so little practical use of it? For he knew James Lang to be a reasonably prosperous landowner.

Obviously the room was seldom used. The fire in the totally inadequate fireplace had probably been lit in the last half hour and did nothing to alleviate the November chill. He remembered how Inez had looked when she'd first returned home—thin, grey-faced. But how she had bloomed again in the climate of her mother country, so that now she looked almost a younger woman than the one who had deserted James Lang and her elder daughter. But of course, there were other reasons, besides climate, for that transformation, he thought wryly.

And this must be the elder daughter. *Deus,* but she was tall, nearly as tall as he. She had inherited her father's bones, as, of a certainty, she had inherited that head of glorious red-gold hair, which she wore in an unsuccessful attempt at a chignon.

Her father's height, her father's colouring, but despite the shapeless tweed skirt, the bulky woollen sweater—he recognised the necessity for it in this house—her slim figure could not be entirely disguised and her poised, graceful carriage was that of Inez, as were the grey eyes, the soft contours of her full mouth.

But James Lang's daughter was far lovelier than her mother had ever been, than her younger sister promised to be. However, it often resulted thus, the mingling of blood and cultures.

'Philippa?' He used the good Portuguese name her mother had given her, not this absurd English contraction her father had used. What was it? Pippa?

She moved towards him, her manner composed, her slender hand outstretched, but as he extended his own, he paused, his dark azure eyes puzzled. Then he drew in a sharp breath. *Deus,* but the Fates played a tricky hand.

He had not recognised her at first. Six years had wrought many changes. But he knew he had met her before, this coolly composed young woman, and then she had been neither cool nor composed and he had almost certainly, he thought, saved her life!

His musical, faintly accented voice made her name sound strange, yet oddly beautiful—exotic, Pippa thought. But then there was something exotic about him, too.

She wasn't sure what she'd expected, but it hadn't been this. Her grey eyes travelled upward with increasing incredulity.

Carlos de Alvarez was tall—very tall—muscularly but sparely built, with a lean intelligent face—a swarthily complexioned face that must, she thought, need shaving three or four times a day. His chiselled features were singular, too individual perhaps to be called handsome, the whole giving a sense of almost monastic asceticism. Only the mouth denied that impression, the lower lip full, sensual.

She felt a nervous tingle run the length of her spine as she, who admired no man, acknowledged that he was really something.

Unusually for so dark a man, he had blue eyes, which, at the moment, were studying her with something approaching shocked surprise. His tall figure had stiffened into stillness, his well shaped mouth was tautly compressed, and she had the distinct impression that the nostrils of his quite perfect nose were flared in some distaste—a distaste for which she could not at first account.

A polite smile had curved her lips—after all, this man was a distant relative. The smile made her already lovely features quite spectacular. But then, as they studied each other, the recognition became mutual, her smile faded and with a little gasp, she withdrew her still outstretched hand.

'You!' she said accusingly. 'Oh no! What are *you* doing here? You can't be ...? Are *you* ...?'

She had never expected to see the man again. To be more precise, she had hoped devoutly never to see him again. Viewed in retrospect, from the viewpoint of greater maturity, her behaviour then appalled her, the circumstances of their encounter embarrassed her. Her recollection of her *naïveté* was humiliating.

Until the age of nine, Pippa had known her mother's firm rule. Volatile of temperament, Inez Lang had been by turns sulky, demonstratively affectionate, sometimes harsh towards her children, and Pippa, as the elder, had borne the brunt of these swings of mood. Whilst she could now recognise those moods as the outward signs of Inez's unhappiness with her lot, at the time she had been upset and bewildered by her mother's changeable nature, her strictness.

Discipline, Pippa's in particular, had been a frequent source of disagreement between James and Inez. Inez herself, raised in a regime of narrow severity, had shown that same severity towards her daughter. The mild-mannered James had advocated a gentler, more loving rule.

'She's only a child!' Pippa could remember hearing him say. And after Inez had left him, Pippa's more relaxed upbringing had demonstrated his liberal views.

Thus, with no mother to guide or supervise her, the young Pippa had been allowed the freedom to come and go much as she liked. Her scholarly father, engrossed in his books, and in any case with no idea of how to approach such intimate subjects, had given her no guidance in the choice of her friends, nor had he sought to enquire into her behaviour, or instruct her in the facts of life.

As she reached her teens, of course, the giggling speculations and confidences of her peers had left her in little doubt on that score. But knowledge in itself proved to be no protection against experience.

Peter Makin, a young Londoner visiting a relative in Little Pennyfeather, and with time to kill, had seemed very glamorous to the unsophisticated, somewhat lonely teenager, separated by school holidays from her classmates. Tall, blond, amusing, he had been the epitome of all her girlish imaginings and in no time at all, Pippa was wildly infatuated. That was all it had been, she later acknowledged, infatuation. But then the sensations she had felt in his arms had been new and exciting. Innocently, she permitted increasing familiarity and, carried away by these sensations, conscience momentarily dulled, she had allowed the final intimacy.

Those few moments of euphoria had been succeeded by the guilty knowledge that she should not have behaved so—and it was as well for her resolution not to allow a repetition of the incident that, very soon afterwards, Peter Makin left Little Pennyfeather—and Pippa was able to push the affair to the back of her mind, where it might have remained but for an overheard conversation.

The servants tended to overlook the presence of their employer's young daughter, speaking freely in her hearing on many matters. On this occasion, the kitchen staff were discussing the local butcher's daughter, much admired and sought after by the village lads.

'Done it once too often did young Hannah,' the cook pronounced, with prurient relish.

'Did what?' the maid, a girl younger than Pippa, asked.

The cook enlightened her in graphic terms, adding the rider,

'And now she's pregnant. Butcher chased her all round shop with his cleaver when he heard. Well, it'd be a shock to any father, wouldn't it?'

As usual, no one had noticed Pippa's presence and she crept out of the kitchen and up the back stairs to her room, her panic-stricken brain digesting what she had just heard.

Certain of the crude words the cook had used were unfamiliar to her but she'd heard enough to convince her that, like Hannah, she too could become pregnant. Pippa's father might not pursue *her* with such violent intent as the butcher had chased his daughter, but James's sorrow, his bitter disappointment in her would be as hard to bear as anger.

A medical book supplied any details she lacked and when her period was several days late, she had no further doubt.

There was no woman in whom she cared to confide. Had this been term-time, she thought, she might have ventured to speak to one of her teachers. But Pippa was not lacking in courage or common sense and, however little she relished the idea, she knew the sensible thing to do was to approach her father. That evening, after dinner, she sought him out in his study.

She sensed she did not have her father's full attention, as he looked up from his farm accounts.

James, as he freely admitted himself, had not been cut out to be a farmer. He had been happy up at Oxford, reading the Classics, confident that, as a younger son, he would be allowed to remain a perpetual student. His older brother's death, only months prior to that of their father, had presented him with an inescapable duty, that of looking after his mother—still at that time alive—and that of running the estate. These days he could leave most of the day-to-day organisation to his farm manager and a capable staff, but the overall responsibility for correspondence, for checking the accounts, he could not escape.

'What is it, Pippa?' His tone was kind enough, but she sensed his impatience. 'I want to get through this mound of paperwork tonight, and I'm expecting a damned nuisance of a visitor any minute. Incidentally, Pippa, I want you out of the way while he's here, OK?'

Pippa didn't query this statement. She was accustomed to making herself scarce when business was being discussed.

'So what is it? More pocket money?'

'No, of course not.' Even as a child, Pippa had been thrifty. 'But there's something I have to tell you, Dad. I don't know who else to tell. I'm afraid you're going to be very angry with me.'

She dared not watch her father's face as she stammered out her pitiful little tale, but when, at the end of the relation, there was total silence, she looked up to witness the conflicting emotions that ravaged James Lang's face—a mixture of anger, sorrow, self-blame.

'Who's the man?' he demanded, then, before Pippa could speak, 'If your mother were here, she'd be in a marvellous position to say "I told you so". I've been lax, criminally lax, but then, dammit, *she* should have been here to give you the guidance a girl needs. I . . .'

But a hesitant knock on his study door interrupted that first moment of painful knowledge, and a maid appeared sufficiently to announce, 'The foreign gentleman is here, Mr Lang.'

'My God!' James struck his fist upon his desk in a resounding blow. 'What a damned coil! Look, Pippa, we'll sort this out, but we can't discuss it now.' He gestured towards the french windows. 'Go that way, will you, and don't come back until I've got rid of this fellow.'

Her father had a right to be furious with her, Pippa thought, not recognising that most of his anger was directed at himself. She hurried to do his bidding. She supposed she ought to be glad of this reprieve before summary justice was dealt her, but somehow she would rather have had it over there and then, to have heard what solution her father could offer to her problem.

Not really aware of the direction in which her feet were taking her, Pippa remained lost in thought until she reached the riverside, a favourite childhood haunt.

The late summer day was on the edge of darkness as she idled along the bank and even her self-preoccupation could not blind her to the river's beauty, the last of the sun's rays gleaming on the rippled surface, the weeping willows trailing dilatory fingers in the water.

Pippa's favourite place for quiet reflection was beneath the green umbrella of one such willow, and she edged her way down the sloping bank to reach a stony outcrop between the tree's roots. She didn't cry, hers was not an hysterical nature; but she couldn't be sure afterwards how long she had sat there in troubled thought, though a fingernail sliver of moon was riding high in the sky when she rose, stretching cramped limbs.

Rain from the previous day had softened the riverbank and, less sure-footed than usual, Pippa felt herself slipping backwards. As she plunged into the water, she let out a little cry—not of fear—but of surprise and outrage. Normally she was not careless or clumsy.

A tall man striding along the river's edge, had heard the cry and the splash and, heedless of his immaculate, well-tailored suit, plunged down the bank to her rescue.

The water at the river's edge was not deep, for here the bank shelved, but it was thick with mud and weeds and his trousers were saturated to the knees when he emerged dragging Pippa, his hands beneath her armpits.

'*Madre de Deus*! What is it you are trying to do?'

'I'm not *trying* to do anything,' Pippa snapped. Her teeth were chattering, not with cold but with shock, and his peremptory tone irritated her, especially since there had been no need for his precipitate action. Though, she admitted, he had obviously meant well. 'Thank you very much for your help,' she forced herself to say politely, 'but you needn't have bothered.'

'You didn't *want* my help?' He sounded incredulous.

'No!' Pippa retorted. She knew she had been in no danger, that she had been quite capable of scrambling to safety.

As Carlos studied the girl before him, his blue eyes searchingly intense, he too was remembering that incident six years ago.

He remembered how he'd had to suppress his irritation at his ruined and uncomfortable trousers—and at her ingratitude. He had been annoyed in any case, when he'd set out along what he'd been assured was a short cut to the village hostelry.

The matter was more serious than he'd at first thought. This young woman—her voice sounded youthful and his experience told him that the body his arms had briefly encircled had been immature—this young woman was in some kind of trouble. She had thrown herself into the river and, but for his presence, might now have been drowned.

True, it was none of his business, but it was only common humanity to talk with her, to reason with her, to steer her away from her dreadful intent.

'You are worried about something?' he suggested gently.

'Yes!' The girl had sounded surprised at his insight.

'You would like to talk about it, perhaps? Ask advice?' He had waited tensely, striving to see her face as she considered the idea, could only guess at the thoughts racing through the youthful brain.

'I'm pregnant,' she said with sudden, blunt confidentiality. 'And I don't know what to do. And my father . . .'

'*Deus*!' But Carlos de Alvarez had suspected something of the sort. 'Your father will not help you? Your mother?' As he spoke, he grasped her arm and marched her briskly away from the source of temptation—the river.

'My parents are separated. My mother lives abroad. And when I told my father . . .'

'He was angry! *Santos*, I am not surprised. But he *is* your father. Of a certainty, he will call upon the young man's parents—insist that you be married?'

'Oh, no!' There was no mistaking her horror at this idea. 'I don't love him—I know that now. And besides, I don't even know where he lives. He was just a summer visitor.'

This was getting beyond Carlos's experience. In his country such things did not happen—at least not in the stratum of society to which he belonged. He marched Pippa even faster.

'Do you even know the young man's name?' he enquired, with a trace of irony.

'Of course I do. It's Peter—Peter Makin.' She had missed the irony and her tone was ingenuously frank.

'I shall see you to your home,' Carlos announced. 'And you will talk more with your father. He will still be angry, yes, but then gradually the anger will be less, and when it is so, he will help you.'

'Do you really think so?' In the faint light shed by the moon, the girl peered up at him.

'I'm certain of it,' Carlos said with more confidence than he felt. Not knowing this child's father, how *could* he be sure? But, at all costs, she must be deterred from the dreadful course she had taken once already tonight.

They were passing the church now and its floodlit façade reflected light back on to the faces of the man and the girl. Carlos stopped, taking advantage of the illumination to study the young face, wanting to be certain that she would take his advice.

Even in immaturity, he noted absently, there was a sure promise of beauty, and he knew he would not easily be able to forget the hauntingly sad features of this child-woman.

'You will do this? You will speak with your father?' he asked, annoyed by the unwilling sense of involvement he felt.

'Oh yes, and you needn't see me any further,' she told him. 'I'll be quite all right now.'

Carlos glanced at the expensive watch that banded his wrist; it was, miraculously, still working after its immersion. It was growing late, and the landlady of the Tar and Feathers had warned him that he would find the house locked up at a certain hour.

'Very well!' He released his grasp of the young arm, but even so he lingered a little. 'But promise me you will never do such a thing again?' This gnawing anxiety for a strange child surprised him.

'I promise!'

Had he thought she was half-witted, or merely promiscuous? Pippa wondered now, as she stared back defiantly into the darkly attractive face. Since she'd had no other course of action in mind, she had promised readily to speak to her father again; and of course she would never repeat her dilemma—get pregnant again. Apart from the fact that she genuinely regretted that moment of madness, Pippa Lang never made the same mistake twice.

Now, how she wished she had never confided in this man! At the time she'd thought it would be a distinct advantage to tell her troubles to a total stranger, someone whose face she could barely distinguish, someone she need never see again. For in a small place such as Little Pennyfeather, she would have known if this man were a regular visitor. And somehow she had sensed her unworldly father's feelings of inadequacy, deciding that it would be easier to return to face him with her own ready-made solution. But now ...

Well, she had kept her promise, Carlos reflected, though at the time, six years ago, it had never occurred to him that she might be James Lang's daughter, access to whom had been denied him, which had been the reason for his anger as he strode along the river path.

Had her pregnancy gone full term? If so, he wondered what had become of the child—Inez's grandchild, bearing the blood of de Alvarez! How would Inez take that information? How was he to tell her what he had discovered? Would she even care? As these thoughts raced through his mind, James Lang entered the drawing-room.

'Ah, there you are, Pippa. I've been looking for you. Well, Senhor de Alvarez, what have you to say to my daughter? I must remind you, messages from my wife are unwelcome in this house.'

'To *you* also?' Carlos asked the girl who was still regarding him with troubled eyes, such large grey eyes, with darker flecks in them, increasing rather than detracting from their beauty.

'I—I should quite like,' Pippa said, after a hasty glance at her father, 'to hear how my mother is. But I thought she had forgotten all about me?'

'Not so!' Carlos de Alvarez exclaimed. 'Six years ago, I came to you with the message I bear today, but at that time your father was not willing for you to hear it.'

'Dad?' Pippa turned towards James Lang, questioningly rather than reproachfully. Now she knew what Carlos de Alvarez had been doing in Little Pennyfeather all those years ago.

'You were under age,' James said defensively, 'I thought it for the best—besides,' with greater firmness, 'as your legal guardian I was within my rights ...'

Even had his mind *not* been made up long before de Alvarez arrived, James pondered, his daughter's disastrous confession at that time had made him more *distrait* than usual and more discourteous than he might otherwise have been to his wife's relative.

But mingled with the anger and distress he'd felt had been an aching compassion for his daughter. Himself a sensitive man, he had recognised the fear, the shame that distorted her young face, had recognised that she had come to him as her only resort. Pippa had had no idea, he'd realised afterwards, that his anger was directed not against her, but against the man who had deflowered her, against himself for his neglect, against his wife for her dereliction of duty.

'How is my mother?' Pippa asked de Alvarez. 'And my little sister?'

'Not so little now,' Carlos told her. 'Last week Mariana celebrated her eighteenth birthday. Your mother is in good health. It *was* her wish—our wish— that I invited you to accompany me back to Portugal, to my family home, but . . .' He hesitated.

'But?' Pippa's usually low, measured tones rose slightly in enquiry as she sensed his reservation.

'You have perhaps a husband to be consulted?' Carlos hinted.

Since he had failed to take her outstretched hand, it had remained with the left, clasped behind her back, so he could not see if she wore a ring.

'No. No husband. I'm a free agent!'

'I thought you might be married now—*with children*?' He emphasised the words.

At that instant, Pippa realised exactly what he was implying, what he was asking, and she felt her temper rising. Now she could interpret the look of shock and distaste with which he had recognised her. Inez de Alvarez's elder daughter would have been welcome, a suitable guest in Carlos's family home, had she not also been the girl he'd rescued from the river, the girl who had ingenuously confided her fears to him. He was not to know . . . Despite her tight control, there was a distinct edge to her voice.

'As I said, Senhor de Alvarez, I'm a free agent!'

So what had she done? Carlos brooded. Taken advantage of the barbarous custom of abortion now practised so freely? Or, less blameworthy, given up her child for adoption?

'Which is why,' Pippa continued, her chilly tone in direct contrast to the smouldering anger within her. 'I'm refusing your invitation.'

'Good girl!' James Lang broke in, but his gratification was short-lived.

'I've a prior commitment—to my employer. I expect to be travelling extensively with *him* in the very near future.'

'In what capacity?' The question was rapped out before Carlos could check it, or the ironic tone in which it was issued, and the perfect face before him flamed scarlet.

'That, Senhor de Alvarez,' Pippa snapped, 'is none of your damned business!'

CHAPTER TWO

'AND am *I* allowed to enquire?' James Lang asked his daughter, after Carlos de Alvarez had left. His expressed regrets at Pippa's refusal to accompany him to Portugal, she thought, had been all too patently insincere.

'Of course, Dad! Monty's asked me to travel with him. He's suddenly decided he needs fresh inspiration for his writing. He wants me to do the usual research.'

'I see!' James wondered why his daughter hadn't simply told that de Alvarez fellow that she was Monty Mortimer's assistant, that the eccentric author was far too old to represent any danger to her virtue. Not that James had any objection to Pippa's reserved manner with the Portuguese. Inwardly, he applauded the way in which she had given the fellow his *congé*. 'And when do these literary peregrinations begin? Where are you going? I may ask, I suppose?'

Amused by his mild irony, Pippa's features relaxed into a smile. Carlos de Alvarez had angered her, but he was gone, the incident over.

'I've no idea. I wish I had. Perhaps Monty will tell me when I go up there tomorrow.'

With an object in view, in this case the furtherance of her own ambitions, Pippa could be doggedly persistent and three years ago, with no little ingenuity, she had contrived the apparently impossible, a meeting with Little Pennyfeather's local celebrity—a determined recluse—the writer Montague Mortimer.

She had been fortunate. A whim had inclined him to listen, albeit patronisingly, to some of the work of this aspiring young author and—to Pippa's everlasting surprise—he had suggested that she take employment with him on a dual basis—she to be his secretary and research assistant, he her mentor.

Thankful for the secretarial course her father had suggested she take—in the vain hope that Pippa might take an interest in the farm office—she had worked with Monty for three years now and was flattered by his condescension towards her, his reliance on her ability to straighten out his more convoluted sentences, to order his somewhat eccentric grammar.

Recently, Monty had shown signs of *ennui* with his self-imposed reclusiveness. He needed, he told Pippa, fresh scenes to stimulate him, and to that end he proposed to travel, proposing furthermore that Pippa should accompany him; and, from the preparations he had been making recently, Pippa guessed that the first of their journeys was now imminent. She had taken care to see that her own passport was up-to-date and now she eagerly awaited the moment when Monty would deign to tell her their destination.

'It's all arranged, dear girl.' Monty adjusted his monocle, an affectation he preferred to spectacles, to look at her. 'We leave on the fifteenth of the month.' He was in high good humour. Usually his long face with its deeply cleft cheeks had a sallow cast, but now it was flushed pink with anticipation.

'So soon!' Pippa exclaimed. 'But that's next week!'

'What do you mean—so soon?' Monty looked sulky. 'I thought you were wild to go? Of course, if you'd rather I found someone else . . .?' He knew he was safe in making this threat, or he would never have risked it.

'Of course not, Monty. It's just that—well, I don't even know *where* we're going, so I don't know what clothes I might need.'

'Take the bare minimum,' Monty said loftily, 'we'll shop when we get there.'

'*Where*?' Pippa cried in some exasperation.

'No!' Fretfully, Monty snatched at his monocle, which in moments of stress always slipped from its insecure position. 'I want no one, but no one, to be told my exact whereabouts. I will *not* be hounded to death by reporters.' And Pippa had to admit that Monty Mortimer coming out of his long seclusion would certainly be a newsworthy item.

'But I promised Dad I'd give him an address where he could contact me if necessary,' she protested, 'and he isn't likely to tell the Press . . .'

'One can't be too careful,' Monty insisted. 'Now, do be a good girl and stop worrying me. Can't you see I have a thousand things on my mind? Take some time off— take as much as you like—go shopping, but be ready for the fifteenth.' As a grudging afterthought, 'You can have an advance on your salary—if you like?'

'That's very generous of you, Monty,' she said drily, 'but I think I can manage.'

He missed the irony, Monty treated financial matters seriously.

'Generous be blowed!' he snorted. 'I don't throw my money around. You'll be earning it in the next few months.' His pale yellow eyes glazed over and he clasped his hands ecstatically. 'Oh, how I shall work in such surroundings! And,' his gaze returned to Pippa, 'how *you* will work!'

Pippa didn't doubt it, but she didn't mind. It was all experience, all grist to her own particular mill. One day, she promised herself, the name Philippa Lang would be as famous, if not more so, as that of Montague Mortimer, and in the meantime she would show her gratitude for the chance he was giving her by working as long and as hard as even his demanding nature could require.

If Monty felt a pang of conscience, he didn't let it trouble him, though he was well aware that Pippa's sense of her good fortune in obtaining the notice of such a distinguished man of letters had blinded her to the truth. Increasingly, her style, her ideas, were being imposed upon the great man's. He, whose candle of inspiration was beginning to burn low, was depending more and more upon her fresh young imagination, her enthusiastic energy for many of the ideas he claimed as his own. He was well aware of the staleness of his mind, and not a little alarmed to find just how much he did depend upon Pippa.

'Sorry, Dad! But dear old Monty is still adamant,' Pippa told James the night before her departure. 'All he'll tell me is that he's roped in some distant relative of his, a nephew I think, to act as our courier. But don't worry, I promise I'll write the very first chance I get, to let you know where I am.'

November in Lisbon held the lingering warmth of summer, far removed from the winter chill of Suffolk. In front of the fine airport, rows of taxis were parked in

the shade of dark-leaved orange trees. The airport was so
close to the town that almost before Pippa had realised it,
they were driving under the branching trees of the
Campo Grande.

Beyond the park and between the tallest houses, the
town lay before them like a spring garden, the house
fronts painted in flower colours, pinks and white,
yellows and greens.

But Pippa was in no mood to appreciate the beauty or
the novelty of her surroundings. In the space of the last
few hours she had received two distinct shocks.

The first had come when she and Monty were met at
Heathrow by Monty's chosen courier, his nephew, and
she'd discovered that he was none other than Peter
Makin. While Peter had registered only mild surprise,
she had been unable to disguise her start of horror, as she
recognised the tall, blond young man.

'Well, who'd have thought it!' Peter exclaimed.
'When the old boy said one of the local girls was acting as
his assistant, I never dreamt it would be you. Small
world, isn't it?'

And Little Pennyfeather was only a moderately sized
village, Pippa thought wryly, but of all the people living
there Peter could have been related to, it had had to be
Monty; and she realised just how little of their previous
acquaintance had been spent in conversation, otherwise,
surely, she would have known?

'And *I* didn't know Monty's nephew would turn out
to be *you*,' she said sharply.

'Whoops! Do I detect a note of displeasure?' Peter
asked with the grin that had once had the power to melt
her bones. 'I always thought you were rather fond of me.
What did I do?'

'Nothing,' Pippa said hastily. 'It—it was just that I didn't ever expect to see you again.'

She could scarcely explain to Peter that, six years ago, she'd convinced herself she was pregnant by him.

She'd realised her mistake only hours after her mishap in the river. If only she'd waited a little longer before pouring out her fears to her father, they would have been naturally resolved. As it was, despite his relief—or perhaps because of it—James, though such behaviour was alien to his nature, had subjected her to a long, angry harangue on her conduct, and it had been some time before he relaxed his vigilant surveillance of her comings and goings.

'I must say it's great to see you again, Pippa,' Peter told her as he escorted her and his uncle out across the tarmac. 'You didn't know Pippa and I had met before, did you, Uncle. I'd forgotten just what a cracker she was. We had quite a thing going for us. I'd always intended to come back, but somehow . . .' He shrugged.

'Somehow, it hardly seemed worth it,' Pippa finished for him, her voice tart, 'for the sake of a schoolgirl five or six years younger than yourself.'

'Hey!' Peter broke stride to look at her. 'You really cared didn't you?' Complacently, 'Well, there's no reason why we shouldn't get together again this trip.'

She'd given him a totally wrong impression, Pippa thought in dismay, but any set-down she might have contemplated was stillborn as she received her second shock of the day.

'We're not going on *this* flight, are we?' The aeroplane towards which Peter was steering them bore the slogan Air Portugal.

'Of course!' Peter sounded surprised. 'Didn't you know?'

'No, I didn't.' She turned to Monty. 'Why Portugal?'

'Why not?' he demanded irritably, fielding his monocle with less than his usual expertise. The exigencies of travel were already beginning to tell on the elderly recluse. 'What's wrong with Portugal, pray?'

'Nothing, I suppose,' Pippa said doubtfully. After all, she told herself, surely Portugal was a large enough country to make minimal the chances of her encountering Carlos de Alvarez.

Though she was curious about Portugal and its part in her ancestry, Pippa realised she had never really forgiven her mother for leaving; and although time had deadened the pain of that desertion, she felt she did not want to see Inez again. But in any case, now she had met Carlos de Alvarez, his recognition of her had put paid to any further invitations.

Purposely, she hadn't told Monty about his visit. The merest suggestion that she might have asked for time off to go to Portugal would have thrown Monty into a ferment of agitation. 'A day not spent in writing is a day wasted' was his favourite maxim, especially where it concerned his own work. Pippa had little time to further her own ambitions, mainly because of the hours she spent polishing and perfecting Monty's writing.

The discovery of their destination had spoilt Pippa's enjoyment of the flight and she had scarcely listened to Peter's complacent reminiscences about their former friendship, a modified form of which he was retailing to Monty's, for once, attentive ear. As a general rule, Monty heard only what related to or might benefit himself.

The taxi deposited them outside the hotel Alfama and Pippa found herself swallowed up in the unaccustomed, unbelievable sumptuousness of gilt, plush furnishings, crystal chandeliers and air conditioning. The suite of rooms Monty had reserved for his party had a panoramic view across the Eduardo the Seventh Park.

'This must be costing him a fortune,' she commented to Peter, as they awaited Monty in the hotel's top-floor restaurant.

'Not really.' Monty's nephew shrugged laconically. 'I work for Travelways, a London-based firm. I booked the trip in my own name, at staff discount. Besides, for one night, the old boy can well afford it.'

'One night! But what then?'

'Apparently, he has a very good friend on whom he proposes to park himself for the duration—an open invitation it seems—any time he finds himself in Portugal.'

'That was a pretty safe invitation.' Pippa smiled at the thought. 'This must be the first time in twenty years he's left Little Pennyfeather. He sends me all over England instead.'

Next morning they left Lisbon, Peter driving the hired car, another uncharacteristic expense, which was accounted for when Monty said airily, 'You can return the limousine in a day or two, Peter, on your way back to London. Once we've settled in at the Quinta, I feel sure a car will be put at my disposal.'

Pippa was relieved to hear that Peter wasn't staying long. Whatever he might think, she had no desire whatsoever to take up their former relationship.

She found the drive fascinating. So this was her mother's country, the country of Carlos de Alvarez too.

Strange how she couldn't get the wretched man out of her mind. Those dark, haughty features seemed to be permanently imprinted there.

After some twenty-six kilometres, Pippa was aware of a sudden complete change in climate and vegetation, from barren stony pasture to a lushly cultivated Eden. It was fresh and cool up in the sea-misted hills. Their route, lined with eucalyptus and giant magnolia trees took them past many fine country houses. Fantastic follies and gazebos, crowning every hilltop, caught her fascinated gaze.

The road climbed a tree-clad escarpment that seemed to rise straight up out of the plain, then wound through a village of colour-washed houses that clung to the mountainside. A porcelain-blue tiled church lent piquancy to the narrow streets lined with the intricately patterned tracery of latticework doors. On the north side of the church, a narrow tree-embowered alleyway led upwards still and, at the top, a sign proclaimed that they were now entering the grounds of the Quinta de Estrella—'Privado'.

Huge umbrella trees lined a drive-way that swept up to a long, low house. The Quinta—an exquisite example of rococo architecture with graceful semicircular wings springing out from the main block—was built around three sides of a great courtyard. Together with its outbuildings, it seemed to Pippa that it crouched in a fold of the surrounding protective hills. The upper storey of the white façade was decorated with medallions of classical scenes, accented with granite festoons, and towering above the rooftops were immense yews that gave promise of a mature garden beyond.

'I'm impressed!' Peter gave a long low whistle. 'Your

friends must be rolling in it, Uncle.'

Monty made no reply. He seemed to be in a great hurry now to hustle Pippa out of the limousine, and towards the ornate portico of the house, where already someone was waiting to greet them.

A sense of reserve would have made Pippa hang back. After all, these were Monty's friends. She was only here on sufferance as his secretary. She was aware suddenly of her travel-creased slacks and blouse. The women who awaited them wore graceful, pastel-coloured dresses.

But Monty's well-tended hand had her elbow in a surprisingly strong grip, as he swept her forward and up the shallow steps. It was just as well his grip was strong, for, as Pippa encountered the gaze of one of the women, she gasped and would have stumbled but for his support.

'*Mãe*?' She had been taught to call Inez this, the Portuguese for mother. 'What's going on?' she asked indignantly. 'I had no idea ... Monty?' She looked accusingly at her employer.

'Explanations later, *amada*.' Inez de Alvarez stood on tiptoe to kiss her elder daughter, with apparent affection. How sincere, Pippa wondered, was her mother's greeting? 'And see, here is Mariana waiting to greet you also.' After so many years spent in England, Inez's accent was almost perfect.

Surprisingly, thirteen years had not substantially altered Inez de Alvarez. She was a little plumper of course, but no grey had been allowed to mar the dark hair, her complexion was still unlined. But Pippa would never have recognised Mariana, unless it were for her likeness to her mother.

In contrast to Inez, Mariana was soberly dressed in grey. She was shorter even than Inez and she too had a

tendency towards plumpness, but in the oval, creamy,
olive face, the cool grey eyes, the smooth dark hair, there
was a striking resemblance. Mariana's neat chignon
made Pippa acutely aware of her own ineffectual
attempts at the style. For her red-gold hair, like her
father's was thick and rebellious. But if Pippa was
curious about her sister and pleased to see her again, she
had the feeling that Mariana was less than overjoyed.
After that first glance, the grey eyes were downcast, the
full mouth drawn in a tight line.

'Come in, my dear Monty,' Inez said, 'you are very
welcome, all the more so for having brought my
daughter to me. And this is your nephew, I believe?'

As she spoke, Inez glided ahead of them into the
coolness of a mosaic-tiled hallway. Splendid archways
gave Pippa glimpses of the rest of the ground floor
interior, which seemed to consist of a series of large but
charming rooms, with beautifully painted and tiled
walls.

The *sala*, in which they were finally invited to seat
themselves, was carpeted and painted in pearly grey,
except for one wall—a glazed expanse of yellow *azulejos*
in formal designs. Two long looking-glasses flanked
exquisite Chinoiserie panels, and the furniture Pippa
recognised as Hepplewhite.

'Such a pity I didn't know exactly when you would
come,' Inez told them, 'or you could have travelled back
with my cousin, Carlos. He is in England at this very
moment. He had hoped to visit you, Pippa, while he was
there.' Anxiously, 'You have not seen him?'

'Oh yes,' Pippa said grimly. 'I've seen him. He came
down to Little Pennyfeather last week.'

'*Bom*!' Inez's face cleared. 'Then all is understood. He

invited you to come to Sintra, but was himself unable to return just yet? So instead, you are escorted by my good friend Monty, yes?' Her manner was animated, totally unlike the sulky moody woman of Pippa's recollection.

'I didn't know you and Monty were friends,' Pippa said, momentarily diverted from her unpleasant recollections of Carlos de Alvarez.

'Oh, yes! Many times, when I found life at the farm insupportable, I would visit him. Monty has the great love of painting, of music. Once, *amada*, I too was a lover of music. But your father, he is not a cultured man.'

'Dad's OK,' Pippa retorted indignantly. 'He may not be keen on music, but he's mad about books. And he's a *good* man.'

'Ah, yes—good,' Inez drawled, 'but so boring.' She shrugged plump shoulders, 'But let us not speak of him. What of Carlos? When does he return? He told you?'

'I know nothing about Carlos de Alvarez's movements,' Pippa said sharply, 'and I've no wish to. In fact, if I'd known Monty was planning to come to Portugal, I'd never have agreed to . . .'

'You would not have wished to visit your own mother?' Inez sounded wounded, just as if *she* had been the injured party all those years ago, Pippa thought ironically. But she felt bound in politeness to deny her reluctance.

'It's not that—it's your cousin, Carlos. He, well—he doesn't approve of me. He did invite me to come here, but I refused.'

'What is this?' Inez stiffened with annoyance. 'Carlos does not approve of *my* daughter? Why should he not?' She turned to the writer. 'Monty? You knew of this? You did not mention this in your last letter.'

'Of course I didn't know.' Monty was growing restless, fidgeting with his monocle. He was not the centre of attention. 'I didn't even know de Alvarez had been in England. Pippa didn't tell me,' he said accusingly.

'It didn't seem important,' Pippa said truthfully. 'He'd gone, and I just wanted to forget all about him.'

'Well,' Inez said complacently, 'I am sure it was all some great misunderstanding. But you are here now, and for as long as you like.'

'For as long as *I* like, surely, my dear Dona Inez,' Monty put in.

'That's true, *Mãe*,' Pippa agreed. 'I *am* Monty's assistant and I'm here at his expense. When he moves on, I shall have to go too.' She didn't want to hurt anyone's feelings, but she did wish devoutly that Monty might be smitten with the desire to move on very soon, from under Carlos's roof. She could only hope that his stay in England would be further prolonged.

But besides her reluctance to spend any length of time in Carlos's home, there was a disinclination for her mother's society. With the sight of Inez, so little changed in appearance, there had been a rush of memory—unpleasant recollections of Inez's strict regime, her fluctuating moods. And what would James think, when she advised him of her whereabouts? He would be hurt by what he could be forgiven for seeing as disloyalty, deception—and Pippa always took care to protect her somewhat vague, sweet-natured father from hurt.

Servants were summoned now, and with the minimum of fuss accommodation was ordered for Inez's guests.

'I will come and talk to you, *amada*, while you unpack,' she told her daughter.

The room allocated to Pippa overlooked the rear of the Quinta, and from her window she could see a delightful topiary garden with balustrades and exquisite statuary, all flanked by the giant yews she had observed earlier. Half-way down the garden, a flight of steps, which broke into two, led to a lower area, a water garden with formal bridges and more statues.

The room itself was unashamedly luxurious, and Pippa could not help making comparisons with the more spartan conditions of her bedroom at home. James Lang preferred to plough his money back into the estate, rather than spend it on what he, with his few needs, called unnecessary embellishments. His only extravagance was that of purchasing antiquarian books.

Pippa's feet sank into pale beige carpet. There were dusky-rose hangings at the windows, matched by the bedspread and upholstery of a comfortable chair. The *en suite* bathroom was decorated in beige and pink, too.

After the room's appointments had been demonstrated, an uneasy silence fell between mother and daughter, a silence finally broken by the older woman, as she toyed idly with the curtains.

'I suppose you have not forgiven me, Philippa, for running away?' The beautiful mouth, so like Pippa's own, twisted in a rueful expression, but Pippa had the impression that Inez did not expect to hear, or much care whether she heard censure from her daughter's lips.

There was something different about this Inez though, Pippa thought; outwardly at least, her manner appeared mellower than Pippa recalled—almost complacent. Perhaps the years had changed her mother?

'When you left I was upset, naturally,' she said finally, 'and I didn't understand, of course. I still don't.'

'Some day, maybe, I will tell you everything,' Inez said carelessly, 'when I think you are capable of understanding, but not now. Now we talk of you, what you have done all these years. I know, of course, of your work with Monty. He has been a faithful correspondent.'

'Yes, I meant to ask you about that. You kept in touch with Monty, yet you never wrote to us—to Dad—to me?'

'I had no wish,' Inez said airily, 'to communicate with your father. It pained me of course, to have to leave you behind. But your father was adamant and I did not wish to spend time fighting him in your English courts. All I wished to do was to return to my home. But tell me now,' Inez went on, 'of all the things I have missed in your growing up. You have had boyfriends, of course? There is a man perhaps in England that you wish to marry?' She sounded as if she would rather this were not the case, Pippa thought, somewhat puzzled.

'No, there's no one.'

She'd been right, for though incredulous, Inez appeared gratified too.

'You have never been in love?'

'Once,' Pippa said shortly, 'or I thought I was. I was wrong. I don't intend to marry—ever. I want a career. *Mãe*,' her face lit up with enthusiasm, 'Monty is teaching me to be a writer. Some day I'm going to be as famous as he is.'

'You will change your mind when the right man comes along.' It was said with confidence.

'No.' Pippa shook her head. 'You thought you'd

found the right man and look what . . .'

'*Não!*' Inez interrupted passionately. 'Your father was never the right man for me—never—never . . . But we will not speak of the past any more, *sim*? You are here now. That is all that matters, and I am deeply indebted to Monty for keeping his promise.'

'You mean—you *asked* him to bring me? It wasn't his own idea to travel?'

Inez shrugged shapely shoulders, amusement lighting her face.

'*Sim*! Monty wanted to travel, but he could not bring himself to endure all the expense—it was ever thus with him. So I say, if he brings my Philippa to me, he can stay here as long as he wishes.'

'And that's why,' Pippa mused, 'Monty wouldn't tell me where we were going. He didn't want Dad to know, in case . . .'

'In case your loyalties to your father were greater than your curiosity to see me,' Inez confirmed.

Such deviousness, on the part of her mother, on Monty's part, was incredible, Pippa thought indignantly. How dared they involve her, however innocent her involvement, in this deception of James? But she was not given time to protest.

'Come,' Inez said. 'There will be a meal prepared for you now, and the good Monty will sulk if I neglect him.'

Throughout the meal, Pippa watched as her mother and Monty chatted animatedly. At first, on hearing of their long friendship, she had wondered if Monty had been one of the reasons Inez had left her husband. But, listening to their conversation, she was reassured. Inez seemed well aware that Monty had no interest in her as a woman, merely as a convenient hostess and an audience for his rhetoric.

Pippa turned her attention to Mariana, on her left.

'It's strange, isn't it,' she said, 'to have a sister you don't really know?'

'Yes.' Mariana's voice was low, expressionless. She still wore the same dark clothes, and her oval face and grey eyes were without animation.

'Well, at least now we'll have a chance to get to know each other,' Pippa persevered.

'Yes.' Mariana remained monosyllabic and, after further unsuccessful attempts to draw out her quiet, remote sister, Pippa turned to listen to what Peter was saying.

'We must do a little sightseeing before I have to get back to London. Lucky you, staying somewhere like this indefinitely.'

'Not indefinitely,' Pippa protested. 'We shall be moving on—and I'm here to work,' she added repressively. She was annoyed at his presumption that she would be eager to spend time in his company. Besides, she knew Monty would be piqued if she were not available when his muse called. But their exchange had been overheard.

'Nonsense, dear girl!' Monty surprised her by saying. 'You must certainly spend some time with Peter. I shall want to look around myself, capture the "ambience" of my surroundings before I can express it in words. Do you know,' he turned to Inez, his manner coy, 'these two young things already knew each other, years ago, and never said a word about it to me until today. Ah,' he sighed, 'young love!'

But Inez's face assumed an expression of total disapproval.

'Monty!' Pippa began, anxious to disabuse him of this notion, but she was not allowed to continue, for Peter seized with alacrity upon his uncle's uncharacteristic laxness.

'There you are you see, Pippa, all settled. Permission from the very fountainhead. We shall explore Portugal!'

They moved back into the *Sala* for coffee, save Mariana who excused herself on some pretext. Although Inez remained well within earshot, Pippa found their party had divided again into two conversational groups, Inez and Monty, herself and Peter, who was once more in reminiscent mood. There was only one way she could put an end to this unwanted tête-à-tête.

'I'm rather tired *Mãe*. Do you mind if I go to bed?'

'But of course not, *amada*.' Immediately, Inez was all concern. 'You must do just as you like. Consider my house yours. You too, Monty,' she added quickly. 'I wish you *all* to live *com familia*.'

Only it wasn't Inez's house, Pippa thought uneasily, as she made her way to her room. It belonged—as of right, her mother had explained over dinner—to the only surviving male member of the de Alvarez family— to Carlos, who, in Pippa's opinion, had been patently relieved at her refusal to accompany him to the Quinta de Estrella.

Probably because she had retired earlier than necessary Pippa was awake early next morning, and she felt a sudden urge to explore on her own. Monty was continually stressing the need to record impressions while they were fresh in the mind, and she knew this would be impossible if she were accompanied by anyone. Swiftly she showered and dressed, then, slipping her notebook—without which she never went anywhere—into her jeans pocket, she left her room by way of the window which opened directly on to a terraced area of garden.

But the garden did not hold her interest for long. Its formality was beautiful, but could have been seen at any of a dozen stately homes Pippa had visited in England. It was the countryside which drew her, and in particular the village she had barely glimpsed on their way up to the Quinta. Having found her way to the main gate, she set out briskly in search of her goal.

On foot it was a greater distance than it had seemed yesterday, but soon she found herself amidst a stream of people heading for the highly glazed tiled church. She had forgotten it was Sunday. Although Inez was a Catholic, Pippa had not been brought up in any particular religious belief, but curiosity drew her to enter the building.

The interior walls, she saw, as she moved into an unoccupied pew, were covered with carved wooden foliage and cherubs in high relief, painted white and gold.

Incense rose in a heady cloud, candles flickered, distorting her vision. The Mass was well and devoutly attended, the sermon obviously powerful in its message, of which Pippa understood little. James Lang had always insisted that his wife speak English with her daughters. Though not surprisingly, Mariana, Pippa had noticed last night, now had a fluency in Portuguese that matched her mother's.

The service over, the worshippers left, but Pippa

lingered. During the celebration of the Mass she had not liked to look too openly about her, but now she could wander at will and she had frequent recourse to her notebook, as she admired the bright blue *azulejos* panels, the ceiling with its painted saints.

Carlos de Alvarez watched Pippa's progress around the church of Espiritu Sancto, the church his ancestors had endowed and of which he was now the patron. From the private chapel the body of the church was not visible, and he had been on the point of leaving when he'd recognised first the red-gold hair, and then the form and features of Inez's elder daughter.

As he drew back out of sight, his first feelings were of anger, his impulse to challenge her, to demand the reason for her presence here—after she had so churlishly refused his invitation. But then curiosity prevailed as to how she would comport herself in this sacred building. He knew from Inez that her daughter did not share her faith. What, he wondered, was she writing so assiduously in the little notebook she carried?

To his annoyance, despite all his efforts, Carlos had been unable to entirely banish Pippa Lang from his thoughts. He had to admit that, despite all his reservations about her character, Inez's daughter had developed into a very lovely young woman, and with her glorious red-gold hair she was intriguingly different from the dark-haired women to whose company he was accustomed. Mariana had inherited the de Alvarez colouring.

Since Pippa had been so adamant in her refusal to visit her mother, Carlos had decided that he would not tell Inez, as yet, what he had discovered about her daughter, about the possible existence of a grandchild. But now—should he not reveal what he knew?

There was his duty to Mariana, too. Philippa would scarcely be a fit associate for her sister, who, since the age of four, had led the sheltered life of the Portuguese women of good family; and, as head of the family, he was the one who should give a ruling on the matter.

But he would not be able to conceal his presence here much longer. The girl was making her way ever closer to the private chapel and he assumed her interest would bring her inside.

Had she been told that here rested the bones of many of her ancestors? Had she realised since her arrival in Portugal just what it meant to be a de Alvarez? Perhaps someone had enlightened her even before she'd left England? Was that why she'd decided after all to come here? Was she avaricious—as well as promiscuous?

As she mounted the two worn, shallow steps that brought her into the chapel, Carlos stepped from the shadows cast by the stone tracery of the screen dividing chapel from church.

Brows drawn together above the finely chiselled aristocractic nose, he confronted her, seeing her start of dismayed recognition.

'And just what brings *you* here, Senhorita Lang?' he demanded.

CHAPTER THREE

HIS words, the austere expression on the darkly complexioned face, struck a chord deep within Pippa. She'd been right about what his reaction would be, if she were to encounter Carlos here on his home territory. He was annoyed. But she hadn't expected to find quite such a violent eruption of antagonism within herself—for that was what it must be, this sensation which made her pulses race, her heart thud erratically against her ribs, while her mouth seemed suddenly parched of moisture.

The striking features which had so impressed themselves on her memory seemed drawn into granite lines, the dark blue eyes appeared hostile. And she hated him, she told herself, hated him because of what he knew about her—or thought he did.

True, he had once been brusquely kind to an unknown girl in distress. But now he knew who she was, he must feel it demeaned him to be related, however distantly, to someone of whom he had such a low opinion.

Well, he needn't worry. She wasn't going to make any claims on their relationship. And as soon as she decently could, she was going to urge Monty to leave the Quinta de Estrella.

But what had happened to the cool manner with which she'd resolved to face this man?

'I—I ...' She was further annoyed to find herself stammering. 'I'm here on business, *senhor*.'

47

His sharp gaze raked the lovely face that her angry colour only enhanced.

'I'm here with my employer,' she went on a little breathlessly, as he made no reply, 'the writer, Montague Mortimer. I'm his assistant. I do his research.'

'And he just "happened" to be coming to *Portugal*? A coincidence?'

'Yes!' she snapped. 'It was just that!' Then she stopped in confusion. It *hadn't* been coincidence, but a plot hatched between Monty and her mother.

His expression of disbelief told her he had noted her confusion and had wrongly attributed its cause.

'I see!' he remarked sardonically.

Pippa was aware suddenly of feeling physically sick, a sensation she attributed to having had no breakfast, and to the startling and exotic form of decoration she had been studying for the past fifteen minutes—the twisting and twining of carved boughs, leaves and flowers. The aristocratic features of Carlos de Alvarez swam before her eyes, against a background of crazy symbolic wreathings of foliage and cherubs.

'I—I should like to leave now, *senhor*,' she said faintly, for he had manoeuvred himself so that he barred her way.

'Why?' he demanded. 'You have not seen all the chapel has to offer—the memorials to your ancestors.'

Pippa had the almost painfully fair complexion of the natural redhead, and in the gloom of the chapel it was not immediately apparent that her face had whitened.

'I—I don't feel too good,' she was forced to admit, though she was reluctant to display any weakness before this arrogant man.

A female ploy? he wondered. But as Pippa crumpled

at his feet, he could no longer doubt the genuineness of her plea. No one, from choice, would fall to these hard stone floors, only narrowly avoiding striking their head on the projecting stonework of a nearby tomb. Because of his surroundings, Carlos stifled the oath that sprang to his lips, as he was obliged to bend and scoop up the limp figure at his feet.

She was no lightweight, this one, he discovered. Tall for a woman, she had also inherited the yeoman ancestry of her father—long heavy bones, not flesh—for though tall, she was supple and slender. And, Carlos thought—unavoidably aware of a full, softly swelling breast just above the firm grasp of his hand upon her ribcage, she had matured considerably since the last time he'd carried her in his arms.

Mariana, he reflected, like her mother, was of much shorter stature and would with time become plump and matronly. This girl would never be that. A light floral perfume assailed his senses and a strand of the red-gold hair brushed his cheek. Annoyed by the trend his thoughts were taking, he hastened his stride, suddenly anxious to be rid of his burden.

As they emerged into the morning air, Pippa's senses slowly returned, though for a moment she could not think where she was, or what had happened to her. Eyes still closed, her natural defences lowered, she was aware of being carried in strong arms that seemed a natural haven, of a vibrantly masculine presence, the unmistakable aroma of an expensive cologne that did not quite mask another less definable scent, the musky not unpleasant aroma of male.

Grey eyes opened wide as full recollection filled her with alarm. Oh God, she thought, panic-stricken, as she

found herself staring into the unfathomable dark face of
Carlos de Alvarez. After a moment's paralysis, she began
to struggle.

'Put me down!' she demanded.

'A pleasure!' With ungallant alacrity, he deposited
her on the sloping grassy bank of the churchyard.

He was staring at her in a most disconcerting way,
Pippa thought, her eyes compulsively scanning the tall
figure in the slate-grey suit. Despite the expensive
tailoring, he was no tame lounge lizard. The cut of his
clothes did nothing to disguise his lean muscularity, his
vibrant sexuality. The dark grey tie, she noted inconse-
quentially, was slightly askew.

'I—I don't usually faint,' she said defensively, as he
continued to look at her, his deep blue eyes inscrutable.

'It may have been the incense. It often has that effect
on people, especially if they're not accustomed to it. You
have not practised the Catholic faith, of course.' Was he
accusing her—as if it were *her* fault instead of her
father's insistence? 'So what were you doing at Mass?'

'I was exploring the village,' Pippa said. She disliked
the advantage he had, towering over her like this, and
she rose to her feet, even though her legs seemed to be
principally composed of cotton wool. 'I saw the people
going in and ...'

'And you were curious?'

'Yes!' she retorted. 'I don't deny my curiosity. What's
wrong with wanting new experiences?'

'It was a "new experience" which once led you into
trouble,' he commented, and as she stared at him
blankly, 'six years ago?'

'Oh!' Pippa gasped. 'You're insufferable. A gentleman wouldn't have—wouldn't have ...'

'Reminded you of your youthful indiscretion? But then it was slightly more than that, wasn't it?' He shrugged. 'However, I suppose our ideas of behaviour and yours are bound to differ. No Portuguese girl of breeding, for example, would have found herself in such a situation.'

About to tell him he was totally wrong about her, a misconception which was her own fault, Pippa bit back the words. After all, she hadn't known six years ago that he would some day turn out to be a relative. It was despicable of him to use privileged information gained accidentally.

'And would a Portuguese girl normally have a mother who deserted her?'

She turned on her heel, not waiting for his reply and walked rapidly away from him, out into the dusty road that led back to the Quinta. But Carlos easily came up with her, laying a restraining hand on her arm, as he halted beside a silver-grey limousine parked outside the church precincts.

She looked pointedly first at him and then at the hand, but he did not remove it.

'You do not like to hear the truth spoken about yourself? Get in!' He nodded towards the limousine. 'I will drive you back to the Quinta.'

Again, Pippa was tempted to tell him 'the truth'. But why should she? Just because a frightened girl had once confided what she believed to *be* 'the facts' didn't make it any of his business here and now.

'It's *you* I don't like, Senhor de Alvarez,' she told him, grey eyes blazing into the blue ones only just above the level of her own, 'and so I'd rather walk.'

His mouth tightened, as did his grasp, and her glare

could not match the intensity of his. Her eyes dropped as he said,

'It will already be known here that you are a guest of the de Alvarezes. You should not be out unescorted. It may give rise to misunderstandings.'

'*More* misunderstandings!' she mocked, though he could not know to what she referred. 'But don't tell me—you're worried about the family reputation.'

'*Sim*, our reputation for hospitality,' he confounded her by saying. 'No guest of ours *walks* to church, least of all a woman. And no Portuguese woman ...' his eyes assessed her figure—despite the tight jeans and T-shirt, or perhaps because of them—obviously feminine and shapely '. . . would appear in a house of worship dressed like that.'

'But then I'm not Portuguese, thank goodness. I'm English and I dress as I like.'

'You cannot deny the Portuguese half of your ancestry,' he reminded her, 'since unfortunately, it exists.'

Unfortunately! Yes. That about summed up his attitude. He deplored her relationship to his family all right. Pippa's dislike of him intensified.

The rest of the household were just assembling for breakfast when Pippa and her unwanted escort reached the Quinta. Thoughtfully, Pippa noted how Mariana's oval face lit up at the sight of Carlos.

'Carlos?' Inez expressed surprise. 'I did not know you were back.'

'I stayed overnight in Lisbon at the apartment, and drove up this morning in time for early Mass. You and Mariana did not attend, I see.' His words made Inez flush and increased Pippa's fury with him. How dared he censure an older woman, to whom he ought to show respect?

'As you see, Carlos,' Inez said defensively, 'I have guests. But Mariana went to Mass up at the convent.' She turned to Pippa. '*You* have been to Mass, *amada*? I did not think ...'

'Not intentionally!' Pippa said with a defiant glance at Carlos. Who did he think he was—setting himself up as the arbiter of her mother's conscience? But in England, she remembered, Inez had been a most regular attender at Sunday services, only missing in cases of extreme indisposition. Strange that she should not be so assiduous to her devotions now she had returned to her native Portugal. 'I decided to look at the village—and the church. Naturally, not being a complete heathen ...' this for Carlos's benefit, 'I waited until the service was over before I wandered around.'

Though Pippa's appetite was keen—she was used to eating at an earlier hour—she was unable to do full justice to the English breakfast served in deference to the visitors. Servants had been quickly summoned and an extra place laid. Pippa, who last night had been at her mother's right hand, now found Inez's place next to her usurped by Carlos. His proximity made her nervous, as did her conjectures about his thoughts as he looked around the table, his eyes often reflectively upon her and Peter.

Carlos had requested in politely formal tones that Inez introduce her other guests. He acknowledged Monty, Pippa noticed, with all the respect due to an older man and a visitor. Carlos might be annoyed by *her* presence here, but it had not made him forsake the social graces.

'And this is Monty's nephew, Peter Makin.'

'So!' Carlos's eyes narrowed as the introduction was made and he gave a sideways, considering glance at Pippa.

With a sinking heart, she recalled that she had mentioned Peter's name to him—only once—all those years ago, but she had no doubt now that he had remembered it.

'Peter is anxious to see something of the countryside before he returns to London,' Inez went on, apparently unaware of undercurrents. 'Perhaps now you are home . . .?'

'My dear Inez.' This time Carlos did not succeed in concealing his irritation at the invasion of his home. 'I am not running a tourist resort.'

'That's OK *senhor*,' Peter put in quickly. 'We wouldn't dream of bothering you. Pippa and I can manage quite well on our own.'

'*Philippa* is to accompany you?' Carlos said sharply. 'Inez, you were aware of this? You permit it?'

Left to herself, Pippa would have soon depressed Peter's assumption that she would willingly accompany him on his explorations, but Carlos's words annoyed her.

'I was brought up in England,' she told him stiffly, 'it's quite customary there for . . .'

'Oh, I am well aware of what is "customary" in England.' Carlos's dark eyes were intent on Pippa's as he spoke and, annoyingly, she felt herself colouring under their disapproving stare, certain she knew just what he was thinking. 'But I cannot have it becoming known locally that a member of the de Alvarez family is roaming about the countryside with a man, unchaperoned.'

'I am not a de Alvarez!' Pippa pointed out with some heat, but she was ignored.

'Then you will escort them?' Inez said with palpable satisfaction. Why, Pippa wondered, was her mother so keen to manoeuvre Carlos into agreement?

'Why cannot you do so?'

'Because,' comfortably, 'I have placed myself and my limousine at Monty's disposal for the next few days.'

'You will take your maid with you?' The inflexion was that of a question, but Pippa had the distinct impression that it was an order.

'Of course.' To Pippa's disgust, her mother agreed placidly.

Though Pippa had had no wish to spend time alone in Peter's company, she was even more reluctant for Carlos to make a third on their expeditions. She wished she could cry off their daily excursions, but to do so would look very pointed, as she had already expressed a curiosity about the country she had never visited.

In the few days at Peter's disposal, they saw the Paco da Vila, built by the Aviz dynasty, embellished in Moorish style, not the work of its Arab builders but of Manuel the First whose travels in Spain had given him an admiration of horseshoe windows and multi-coloured *azulejos*. They explored and admired the botanical park surrounding the Palacio da Pena.

For some Portuguese, Carlos explained, Sintra was a summer residence only. Others lived there all year round in large houses which possessed their own private chapels and stables.

Pippa might detest Carlos, but she had to admit that

he was an interesting, informative companion, and there was no mistaking his love of his country, his pride in its history. In such a mood, she discovered, he was almost likeable.

Peter, understandably, was reluctant to leave when his few days' holiday came to an end, and said so to Pippa one evening, when—a rare occurrence—they had a few moments alone together in the garden.

'It seems a shame, just when we've got together again, and I don't know when I'll be able to get any more time off.'

'Peter, I . . .' Pippa hesitated, uncertain how to phrase her words, to tell him that she didn't especially want to see him again, that there would be no point in his returning to Portugal on her account, but he didn't give her time to finish.

'Damn it, Pippa!' He flung his arms about her in a sudden gesture which gave her no chance of evasion. 'Do you realise this is only the second time we've been alone? Carlos de Alvarez has been hanging round us all week like somebody's old nanny. What does he think we're going to do, for heaven's sake?'

Pippa knew the answer to that, but she wasn't going to tell Peter. For her own part, she had been half resentful, half relieved at Carlos's chaperonage. At least it had prevented moments like this. For Peter was now becoming distinctly amorous, his mouth and hands seeking.

'Things will be a lot better when you and Uncle leave here. At least de Alvarez can't accompany you all over Portugal.'

'Look, Peter,' she tried again, but this time his lips prevented her speaking, covering hers in a series of heated kisses, which, she reflected clinically as she gripped his shoulders in an attempt to push him away, left her completely unmoved.

It didn't look that way to Carlos, coming upon them suddenly, and he felt waves of anger course through him at the sight of their close embrace. How could she behave like this with the man who had left her in the lurch all those years ago, and whom she had only met again just recently—or had she? Had they kept in touch, planning just such a reunion when she was no longer under her father's jurisdiction—and with the uncle's connivance?

'Philippa!' Uttered harshly, the name held none of the beauty his accent usually gave to it.

Startled by the interruption, Peter released her and they both turned to face Carlos, Peter irritated, Pippa mortified. Though why she should care what Carlos thought . . . She tossed her bright head at him.

'Yes, *senhor*?'

'Dinner will shortly be served and you are not yet dressed.' He looked her up and down, and Pippa became acutely aware of her dishevellment. Peter's attempted caresses had been rough and her struggles had done nothing to improve her appearance.

Secretly, she was glad to have been saved from the impassioned scene, but she would rather her rescuer had been anyone other than Carlos and she was piqued by his imagined right to monitor her behaviour.

'I'll go now. It won't take me long.' She attempted to brush past him and regretted the flouncing gesture, for he seized her arm in a grip that hurt and yet, at the same time, made her shockingly aware of him.

'You do not pay sufficient attention to your appearance.'

'I've never been vain.' Pippa strove for lightness, trying to ignore the touch of his hand which still restrained her, the painful way her heart had begun to pound.

'Vanity is one thing, proper pride is another,' he retorted.

Pippa hurried away, vainly trying to rub the feel of his hand from her arm. She was furious at his utter gall, not only in telling her how she should act, but how she should dress. Yet, mingled with her anger was another emotion she did not care to define, but which made her uneasy, apprehensive about encountering Carlos again, about meeting the critical glance of those dark azure eyes.

Apprehensive or not, she would not defer to him in the matter of clothes. She'd never been over-fond of wearing dresses and skirts. Inez and Mariana had never changed from their simple day dresses in the week she'd been here. If her appearance was good enough for her mother, she thought mutinously, then it would have to be good enough for Carlos.

She discarded jeans and T-shirt, but only in favour of white cotton slacks and a silky shirt in vivid emerald green, whose reflection subtly altered the colour of her eyes. Time was getting short and she abandoned her attempt at a smooth chignon, leaving her hair loose about her face, brushing it until it shone copper-gold.

She was the last down. She could hear the murmur of voices in the *sala*, as the de Alvarezes and their visitors awaited the announcement that dinner was served. Head held high, the gleam in her eyes and the set of her mouth daring anyone, someone in particular, to comment, she walked into the room, a slight break in her step as she took in the scene before her.

Peter, Monty and Carlos—all three were in evening suits and snowy linen. Inez and Mariana were in jewel-coloured *décolletée* gowns that set off their dark handsome colouring.

Pippa knew she was the cynosure of all eyes, but she met those of Carlos de Alvarez with a challenge in her own. However, beyond a tightening of his well shaped mouth, his initial reaction was disappointing. Instead Inez came towards her.

'*Amada*! I am so sorry. I should have told you. When Carlos is at home, we dress formally for dinner. Would you like me to delay the meal, so that you can change?' Of course, this would be the first time Carlos had dined at home since his return from England. On other evenings he had visited neighbours.

'No, Inez!' Carlos intervened. 'Philippa will do as she is—for this evening. I do not think she will make this mistake again.' Oh, he was astute. He had recognised her chagrin at appearing to such disadvantage.

He offered his arm to Mariana and led the little party into the adjoining room. Following with Peter, Pippa raged inwardly. If she'd realised everyone else was going to these lengths, she would have donned evening dress, of course she would. She hated this feeling of looking conspicuous and foolish, and her resentment against Carlos increased proportionately, as, somewhat inconsistently, she blamed him for her mortification.

It was not only the diners who had undergone a transformation. On previous evenings they had eaten simply, without ostentation. Tonight, with the presence of the head of the family, things were very different.

A richly embroidered tablecloth set off the ornate

table settings, the silverware with the family crest embossed, the beautiful ceramic-ware, the lighted candles and flower arrangements.

'Here we believe in feasting the eyes as well as the palate,' Carlos was addressing a sagely nodding Monty, but Pippa felt the comment was also directed at her, that he was implying that *she* did not please his eyes. Illogically that hurt.

Even the food was lavishly presented. Bread had been twisted into knots or modelled into various forms before baking. Rice, garnished with shellfish, was moulded into aquatic shapes.

Between courses, assorted delicacies such as sugared almonds, chocolates and preserved fruits were nibbled. The Portuguese, Pippa decided, must have a very sweet tooth.

The meal over, the ladies adjourned to the *sala*, leaving the men to their port. Mariana, still the solitary, wandered over to the magnificent grand piano and began to play, her execution loud enough cover for the conversation that ensued between Inez and her elder daughter.

'I am sorry, *amada*, that you incurred Carlos's displeasure. I blame myself. In Carlos's absences, Mariana and I have fallen into the way of ...'

'Don't apologise, *Mãe*,' Pippa interrupted. 'He was just being his usual carping critical self. I'm darned if I ...'

'But—you do not *like* Carlos?' Inez exclaimed incredulously.

'No, I don't. And he's got a very low opinion of me.'

'I hope you are mistaken, *amada*.' Inez looked

troubled. 'It is important that Carlos should approve of you.'

'I don't need his approval,' Pippa returned. 'I only wish I need never see the wretched man again. I certainly shan't stay under his roof any longer than I can help.'

'His roof,' Inez said snappishly, and for a moment, Pippa saw the woman she remembered showing through the veneer of serene affection, 'is also the only roof I have. I wish very much that it should be your roof also.'

'In the same tradition as the Spanish "*mi casa su casa*"? That's very . . .'

'*Não*, Phillipa.' Inez was in command of herself again. 'It was not merely a formal expression of hospitality. The Quinta was once the home of my own family. But they are all dead. Thus, as you know, the Quinta belongs to Carlos—the son of a cousin many times removed.'

'Yes, and he "very kindly" gave you a home!'

'*Sim*. It is so. But only on certain conditions.'

'He made conditions?' But Pippa wasn't really surprised. 'That was charitable of him!'

'Practical,' Inez demurred, missing the sarcasm. 'You must remember, Philippa, that our family is an ancient one. We are descended from Jão de Alvarez, a close friend of Pedro the First. We four—you, Mariana, myself and Carlos are the sole descendants of that family—which is why Carlos has sworn to perpetuate the pure line of descent by marrying one of my daughters.'

'How very—feudal.' Pippa's eyes widened in disbelief. 'And he actually made that a condition of your living here?'

'*Sim*. Do not forget, I have no real right to be here. In

his eyes and in the eyes of my church, I should still be under your father's roof. Do not look so horrified, *amada*. Carlos's proposal meets with my complete approval.'

'Poor Mariana!' Pippa exclaimed.

'*Perdão*?'

'Well, it's obvious, isn't it? She's the most suitable candidate? She's lived under Carlos's roof for the last thirteen years. She's used to Portuguese ways—she hasn't earned his disapproval, as I have; and I can tell she likes him, though Lord knows why.'

There was a long silence, then, 'And how about you, Pippa? Suppose it were you upon whom his choice fell?'

'Me?' Pippa laughed with a touch of hysteria. 'I wouldn't marry Carlos de Alvarez if—if I were starving and he owned the last crust of bread in the world. So it's just as well I don't qualify.'

CHAPTER FOUR

'AND why do you think that should be so?'

Carlos had entered the *sala*, the music drowning his footsteps, and a dismayed Pippa, instantly on the defensive, swung around to encounter the derisive glitter of dark blue eyes.

'Because—naturally—the mother of future de Alvarezes must be as above reproach as Caesar's wife!' And as Carlos continued to regard her with an unfathomable expression, neither confirming nor denying her taunt, she felt driven to goad him further, 'And like Caesar's wife, she'll be married to an arrogant dictator. You don't know how glad I am that I *don't* qualify, that the great privilege is going to be Mariana's. I wish her luck. She'll need it.'

'Philippa!' Carlos's tone was warning. 'You will say nothing of this to Mariana. I will advise her in my own good time of *my* plans.'

'I bet you will!'

God, the arrogance of the man! So Mariana would 'be advised', would she? And presumably, she would also be expected to agree without demur to the honour he had in store for her?

Pippa became thoughtful. Mariana might just do that, too. If she read her sister right, the younger girl always seemed very anxious to please Carlos. She felt suddenly, unaccountably sad.

A puzzled Inez had been following their verbal duel.

63

'What does all this mean? Carlos? Philippa? Above reproach? For what should you reproach Philippa?'

Tensely, Pippa waited. Now Carlos had his chance, if he chose to take it. When he didn't immediately speak, she nerved herself to meet his eyes, found their expression puzzlingly enigmatic. She lifted her chin. If he did tell Inez what he believed about her, it would be difficult, but not impossible to disprove.

'Nothing that need concern you, my dear cousin,' Carlos reassured Inez. Then his musical voice became harsh, as he said, 'And now, Philippa, I wish to speak to you—alone.'

'Well, I don't want to speak to you, *senhor*, alone or under any circumstances,' Pippa retorted. 'And you can't order me about as you do my mother and Mariana.'

'Philippa, *amada*, please!' Inez intervened. 'Do not make a scene in front of your sister.' A slight inclination of her sleek head indicated that Mariana had left the piano and was moving towards them, a look of enquiry upon her usually expressionless face.

'Oh, of course not! Mariana must be protected at all costs from her sister's influence!' Pippa was sarcastic.

'They are *your* words,' Carlos said, 'but you are correct—we do not wish Mariana to be exposed to unpleasantness. She is a very unworldly girl. So you will accompany me—if you please!' The polite afterthought was stressed, but it was still a command, Pippa thought resentfully. She doubted if Carlos was accustomed to expressing himself in any other way.

'Please, *amada*!' Inez said again and, remembering that this man had the power to make her mother's life comfortable or otherwise, Pippa bit back the further protests she had contemplated.

'Well?' Truculently, she faced him acros the desk-top of tooled Spanish leather. She hadn't been alone with him since their encounter in the church and, under his gaze, she felt oddly unnerved, threatened.

'Sit down.' A long, lean hand indicated the chair behind her.

'I'd rather stand.' The leather chair would engulf, diminish her.

'Then, if you stand, I must also.' He moved around the desk towards her and though she wasn't quite sure why, Pippa suddenly capitulated. She felt safer with the desk between them.

But to her chagrin, he did not return to the large swivel chair, but sat instead on the edge of the desk, giving him the advantage of height over her. It must be the depths of anger he aroused in her that made his proximity so profoundly disturbing.

'You understand there are questions I must ask you?'

'No, I don't understand. But ask away,' she told him pertly, 'though I won't guarantee to answer.'

He moved restlessly, irritably, and his long leg brushed Pippa's making her jerk away to avoid further accidental contact. She frowned up at him, puzzled by her inner conflict—antagonism mingled with a sensation that was almost—excitement? The adrenalin of anticipated conflict?

'What exactly is your present relationship with Peter Makin?'

At his words, Pippa sat more erectly in the chair, her hands clenching on the coldness of the leather arms. He'd no right to question her about Peter, she seethed. Now she was of age nobody had the right to monitor her friendships.

Well, she'd warned Carlos he might not get any answers and she had the shrewd notion that silence would annoy him far more than an angry retort. She compressed her full lips and deliberately relaxed her body, allowing her eyes to wander around the magnificently appointed library, noting its leather-bound books, the fine oil paintings, the pattern of the embroidered woolrugs scattered about the highly polished floor.

'He *is* the man with whom you had an affair—some years ago?' Carlos persisted. 'You need not deny it. I remember his name.'

Against her will her gaze returned to him.

'Then if you remember, why ask? Anyway, I wasn't going to deny it.' Let him make what he liked of that.

'You have no shame about that incident?' He sounded both incredulous and censorious.

With her lucky escape from any serious consequences of her brief intimacy with Peter, the shame she *had* felt over the incident had faded somewhat. But since this man had re-entered her life, he'd been a constant reminder of that unhappy time and Pippa resented it, his knowledge of her. Why *should* she admit her regret to him? Relation or no, he was not the arbiter of her behaviour. She tilted her chin at him, her lips remaining closed in obdurate silence.

Carlos made a sound of vexation, deep in his throat, but, to her relief, he stood and moved away from the desk, pacing the room, reminding her of some restless, dangerously frustrated animal. 'Philippa, if you remain at the Quinta de . . .'

'But I don't intend to remain,' she interrupted. 'Monty wants to travel and I . . .'

'Does he indeed?' For the first time in their acquaintance Pippa saw Carlos smile, and the experience had the oddest effect upon her, the smile illuminating as it did the dark ascetic features, softening their lineaments, giving the impression of kindliness to a man she already acknowledged as being stunningly attractive. 'That was not the impression I gained from him during our after-dinner talk.'

'Then you gained the wrong impression. Monty's looking for a suitable setting for his next book and . . .'

'Enough!' Carlos said impatiently; the smile had vanished. 'I did not bring you in here to discuss Senhor Mortimer's plans. It is your intentions in which I am interested. Has Peter Makin asked you to marry him?'

Why did he want to know that, for heaven's sake? Unless he thought it was time Peter 'made an honest woman of her'. She repressed the urge to giggle.

At first, she contemplated saying yes. But apart from the fact that she loathed lying, it would be all too easy for Carlos to check. However, without departing from the exact truth, she could give him the impression . . .

'Not yet,' she compromised.

'And if he does? What will your reply be?' He had stopped his pacing so close beside her chair that, although he was not touching her, his warmth was a tangible presence.

'That, *senhor*, is between Peter and me,' she told him demurely.

Carlos held her gaze for a long time and Pippa began to feel uncomfortable, as though he could read her mind, as though he could sense the unaccountable unease his nearness was causing her. Then he shrugged.

'Senhor Makin returns to England tomorrow, so at

least there will be no unsuitable behaviour beneath my roof.' He spoke as if to himself, and before a bristling Pippa could give utterance to her outraged feelings, 'But while you remain here, I must insist that you do not speak of unseemly topics to your sister. She has not been brought up as you have.'

'I've scarcely been allowed more than a dozen words with her unsupervised, so there hasn't been much opportunity to contaminate her! But I promise not to say anything unsuitable for the ears of the future Senhora . . .'

'You speak of things about which you know nothing,' Carlos interrupted her brusquely. 'All I ask is that you do not talk of your past. I have not yet decided whether to tell your mother what I know of you.'

'How dare you! You . . .' Pippa jumped to her feet, eyes blazing silver fire. 'It's not your place to tell her anything about me. If I want her to know, I'll tell her myself.'

'And *will* you tell her? That she has a grandchild somewhere?' His tension as he waited for her answer communicated itself to Pippa.

'Will you stop this—this inquisition!' She was angry—her thoughts in turmoil. Despite her protests at his impertinent probing, she felt an increasingly strong need to vindicate herself, to tell him there had been no child, that she'd done no wrong. Before the urge could overcome her, she turned away, determined, though he had not given her leave, to quit the room.

But he was too fast for her and strong fingers encircled her upper arm, not only preventing her movement but bringing her closer, far too close to his whipcord muscularity.

Unaccountably, Pippa began to tremble. But she wasn't afraid of him, she told herself incredulously. She wasn't!

She had expected a furious refusal to accept her silent defiance, but instead, as she met the probe of azure eyes, she felt his grasp suddenly relax, though he did not release her immediately; and an expression she could not interpret crossed his dark face.

'Very well, Philippa, you may keep your secrets—for the present.'

'Monty!' she said plaintively. 'How long do we have to stay here?' It was the next morning before Pippa could confront her employer. Monty had retired by the time she'd emerged from the library.

'Why?' After three years' close acquaintance, Pippa could recognise his every mood, and knew that he was being deliberately evasive.

'Because I don't think we ought to stay—not now Senhor de Alvarez is home. *He* didn't invite us and ...'

'And you don't like him, do you?' Monty prided himself on his perspicacity.

'No, I don't.'

'Well, that doesn't matter,' Monty told her airily. 'You don't have to like him. Just look upon him as you would any other guide.'

'What do you mean—"any other guide"?'

'I mean that Senhor de Alvarez has kindly offered to escort you on your fact-finding journeys.'

'What do you mean *he'll be escorting me*?' Panic struck at Pippa's throat, so that she had difficulty in speaking. The more she saw of Carlos de Alvarez, the more he worried her and she couldn't think why.

'If you'd just listen, dear girl, instead of jumping down my throat!' Monty swept a well-manicured hand through over-long grey hair, and enthusiasm lit his pale eyes. 'I have an idea for a story—just the teeniest glimmering, you understand—so fragile that I hardly dare breathe it.' Monty had always been adamant that a writer did not speak of his plot during its gestation period. 'Dear Inez has very kindly agreed to introduce me to various people who may be of use to me. Your part, as always, is to research the backgrounds I'll need. I had a list somewhere . . .' He began to rummage through the pockets of his velvet jacket.

'But Monty.' Pippa ignored his distracted gestures for silence. 'If *Mãe* is going to help, we don't need Carlos. She could go with us and . . .'

'Pippa! Pippa!' His expression was pained. '"Us"—aren't we being just a morsel thoughtless? You saw how the flight to Portugal, the journey here exhausted me? I'm not as young as I was. It's very inconsiderate of you to expect me to go tramping about the countryside, writing up material that you can very well gather for me. Oh,' irritably giving up his search, 'it doesn't matter. I gave a copy of the list to the Senhor.'

'Monty, I don't want Carlos standing over me at every turn.'

'Now, don't be naughty, Pippa.' Monty became fretful. 'You know how arguments upset me. I must have tranquillity or my muse will quite desert me. As for de Alvarez, he won't hear of your traipsing around unescorted, so just be a sweet child and do as you're told, hmmm?' Another wave of his hand dismissed her and Pippa knew that the subject was closed, that Monty would refuse to discuss it further.

She recognised another fact too, one which had been all too apparent to Carlos. Monty had never had any intention of touring Portugal. He had found himself a snug little berth here at the Quinta de Estrella and here he intended to remain, his creature comforts well catered for.

Pippa had long been aware that Monty was a parsimonious creature. Normally, out of gratitude for his patronage, she overlooked this fault. But until now, his attitude had never really affected her well-being. Now she would be forced to endure a prolonged stay under Carlos's roof and to accept his company—a thought that was as much disturbing as it was irritating.

How could she be expected to do her best work under such circumstances?

'There's no need for you to get involved, *senhor*,' she told Carlos later that morning, while he studied Monty's list. 'I'm well able to take care of myself, and I'm sure you've got more important things to do.'

Carlos inclined his dark head enquiringly. 'But is it not also important that we get to know each other better?'

'I don't see why.'

'Oh!' He shrugged. 'Shall we say, because you are Inez's daughter? Because whether you like it or not, you have de Alvarez blood?'

'And because I'm Mariana's sister? And you want to know all about the skeletons in the family closet?' Her only reply to this taunt was an annoying quirk of his eyebrows. 'Oh well,' she said irritably, 'come if you must, *senhor*, but you needn't think it's an opportunity for more prying into my private life!'

On the point of entering Carlos's limousine, Pippa looked at him questioningly.

'What, no chaperon?'

'But *we* are related, Philippa!' He sounded surprised, amused. 'Why should we need a chaperon?'

'Oh!' she said in a small voice, feeling foolish. But the only thing that had reconciled her to his arrangement had been the comforting thought of the chaperon. The idea of being quite alone with Carlos all day made her heart thump nervously ...

'What on earth does Monty want to know about this place for?' Pippa gazed around her in bewilderment. The site of the Castelo dos Mouros was overrun by brambles, its stone steps crumbled underfoot, birds nested in the battlements. With its stone walls rising from a natural rampart of rocks, it was a wild still place, lonely, unrelieved in its gloom.

'There is much history here,' Carlos suggested.

'But Monty doesn't write historical novels—or gothics!' Pippa pointed out. 'His books are contemporary—witty sarcastic portrayals of people and their weaknesses. It's me that's interested in history.'

'*Sim*. Your mother tells me you are a writer also?'

'Not yet,' she corrected, 'but,' earnestly, 'I'm going to be.' She looked raptly about her. 'This would make a marvellous setting. Though I honestly can't see why Monty ...' Forgetting her dislike of Carlos, her earlier disinclination for his company, 'Tell me about it,' she demanded, producing notebook and pencil.

'What do you wish to know?' To her surprise, with apparent disregard for his cream-coloured trousers,

Carlos sat down on a grassy bank between the lichen-covered stones.

At his inviting gesture, she joined him, careful to keep a comfortable space between them.

'It is an old Moorish fortress, seventh century. Impregnable, one would have thought, yet it fell, in the twelfth century, to Alfonso Henriques.'

'Alfonso who?'

'Henriques, later Alfonso the First of Portugal—and,' he added as if it had significance, 'the father of Pedro the First.'

'Pedro the . . .? Oh, the Pedro who was the patron of the de Alvarez family!' Pippa said ironically. She disliked snobbery.

'Yes. In thanksgiving for his victory over the Moors, Alfonso built a monastery, at Alcobaça. He also founded the convent which stands on the hillside above the Quinta.'

'Where Mariana went to Mass?'

'*Sim.* Mariana is *beata*—very devout.' There was a ring of genuine affection in his voice as he spoke of her sister, Pippa thought, smitten by an odd twinge of some uncomfortable sensation, which surely couldn't be jealousy? Mariana was welcome to his good opinion.

'Tell me about Pedro,' she prompted, 'not wars, but his personal life.'

'You would write a romance, then?' Carlos seemed amused.

'What's wrong with that, *senhor*?' Was he a literary snob?

'Just that you can know little of such things. Of youth's carnal desires, yes, undoubtedly. But of love, of the grand passions? You are too young. You cannot write about what you do not know.'

'Carnal desires!' Pippa exploded. 'Is that what you . . . you . . . you . . . and how can you be so certain what I do or don't know?' she demanded. 'In any case, I can use my imagination, can't I?'

'Imagination!' He shook his head. 'I doubt if you have it in you to visualise the depths of true love, of obsession, the lengths to which a man will go for the woman he loves. If you wish to write of a man's great love for a woman, you . . .'

'I'd sooner write of a *woman's* love for a *man*,' Pippa retorted, 'it's a far more genuine emotion. A woman wants to feel a mental, an emotional commitment to a man. All a man wants is . . .'

'It is dangerous to generalise, Pippa,' he warned her, 'especially out of your limited knowledge.' He turned on his side to regard her, bringing him closer, making her shiver suddenly. 'Not all men confuse the fact of love with its physical act—as it would seem you once did. You were scarcely idealistic in your relationship with . . .'

'Oh!' She jumped to her feet, glaring down at him. 'I was trying to have a theoretical discussion, but you just can't keep personalities out of it, can you? You have to keep harping on and on—about—about—that time, and you really know very little of . . .'

'I'm willing to hear more,' he suggested. He had risen, too. He was always very punctilious in that respect, she thought resentfully, unwilling to have him show up well in any light.

'Well, you're not going to hear more. Look, I'm supposed to be jotting down my impressions of this place for Monty—and that's just what I intend to do now. I'd be very obliged if you wouldn't distract me.'

'You find my presence "distracting"?' he said interestedly. 'In what way?' He had moved to stand beside her, his arm almost, but not quite, brushing hers. But to Pippa it seemed as though some electrical impulse crossed that infinitesimal gap, as galvanic to her pulses as actual contact. She edged away.

'Only because you won't let me get on with my work.' She was not going to admit, even to herself, that he distracted her in other ways. Away from the atmosphere of the Quinta, where he reigned supreme, Carlos seemed less stiff and autocratic. His manner towards her today had been subtly different.

'I thought you wanted to hear more about Dom Pedro and his love for Inez de Castro?'

'Inez?' Pippa was momentarily diverted.

'*Sim.* Because of her, there has been an Inez in every generation of the de Alvarez family.'

'She was the Queen?'

'His mistress.'

'Oh?' Ironically. 'But surely, *senhor, you* must disapprove of that?'

'Why should I? It is past history. In those days it was well understood that a man must marry for reasons of state, when in reality he loved another.'

'As *you* plan to marry for "reasons of state"?' she mocked.

His brows lifted quizzically.

'Do I indeed?'

'You know you do!' she retorted. 'To keep the de Alvarez blood pure. And will you take a mistress, *senhor*?' she asked, thinking of Mariana, feeling sorry for her in such an eventuality. 'And will your wife "understand"?' She felt an odd little *frisson* of excitement at her own temerity, as she held the dark blue gaze—the surge of adrenalin that seemed always to be present at her encounters with Carlos de Alvarez.

Her eyes did not study his face with more curiosity than that shown by his as he gave her his reply.

'I would have thought my feelings on such a subject must be quite clear to you by now. Naturally I shall be faithful to my marriage vows. You may be quite certain of that.'

'I'm glad to hear it!' she said with sarcastic emphasis. But she was. Though the years of enforced separation had made them strangers to each other, she wished Mariana happiness in her marriage. Pippa's dislike of Carlos mellowed proportionately to his declaration. But one doubt remained. 'What about love? Doesn't that matter to you? There's no love in a marriage of convenience.'

'Perhaps not always—on both sides—in the beginning. But mutual respect can be a good foundation for its growth. Many very happy marriages have grown out of such an arrangement, the partners often finding a deeper, truer love than those based on random selection. The arranged marriage is not a new concept.'

'Exactly!' she said triumphantly. 'It's outdated. Today, thank goodness, women have freedom of choice. I presume that's what you meant by "random selection"? At least,' she amended, 'in England we do. I suppose it's different here? I suppose Mariana will have to do as she's told?'

He did not answer her question. Instead, he said, 'If *you* were married to me, Philippa, do you not believe I could make you love me?'

Startled by the unexpected question, Philippa swallowed. Unaccountably, some obstruction seemed to block her throat, leaving her speechless.

'You seem uncertain?'

Somehow she found her voice. Absurd to feel so threatened by a question that could only be academic.

'Love can't be forced.'

'No? But perhaps it can be cajoled?'

Before she knew what he was about, or could prevent him, strong hands took her arms in a gentle but unbreakable grip, and the Castelo dos Mouros and its environs were blotted from her sight as his dark head came closer and his lips claimed hers in a caress immediately, insistently intimate.

Though the encirclement of his arms was not painful, her struggles proved vain. Inexorably, he pressed kiss after kiss upon her trembling mouth, his tongue probing, and Pippa was not really sure how long it was before she ceased to resist, kissing him back with unbelievable yearning. His kisses were really having the oddest effect upon her, her body reacting to the hard strength of his in a way that surprised her—Peter's kisses had been nothing like this—so that she no longer tried to escape him, but instead longed increasingly for closer contact.

At last he released her and a bemused Pippa stared up at him, colour flooding her cheeks, scarcely able to believe that this had happened to her, that she had actually been kissed by Carlos de Alvarez, that she had kissed him back and, shamingly, had even enjoyed it. And he knew exactly how he had affected her, she thought. There was a look of deep satisfaction in the dark blue eyes quietly studying her, and fury exploded within her as violently as had other sensations.

'You hypocrite!' she hissed. 'You pride yourself on your moral rectitude, your integrity. You claim to be capable of fidelity and yet ...'

'Ah!' It was an exclamation of satisfaction, as he completely ignored her outburst. 'I knew there must be passion somewhere behind that frosty exterior you show me. But I cannot believe that one man—and in particular Peter Makin—taught you all that fire and response. Just how many other men have you "been curious about", Philippa?'

'None!' she snapped, still too furious with him, with herself, to be able to think analytically. Had she been cooler, pride might have made her pretend to be as experienced as he obviously thought her. But in any case he didn't believe her protest, his tone incredulous as he said, 'None? None since that affair with Makin? Or has it been him all the time, for the past six years?' He sounded as if he found it equally impossible to believe her capable of constancy. 'He pays you maintenance for the child perhaps? Where is that child? Why have you never married Makin? Or,' his eyes narrowed, 'is he already married? Like mother, like daughter perhaps?'

'What do you mean?' As he'd spoken, Pippa had tried several times to interrupt, her anger growing with each impertinent question. She'd even been on the point of denying the existence of a child, but this reference to her mother diverted her. 'What do you mean "like mother, like daughter"?'

'I'm sorry.' His tone was curt. 'I spoke in haste. I should not have ...'

The experience of hearing Carlos de Alvarez actually

apologising for something almost silenced Pippa—
almost.

'Well, you *did* speak and I want to know what you
meant.'

'No, Philippa. That is for your mother to tell you—if
she chooses to do so.'

But the diversion, whether or not deliberate, had been
effective. Had it been deliberate, to channel her
energetic anger in another direction? Intentional or not,
she could scarcely return now to the subject of his
having kissed her—not without making the incident
seem important to her.

Verbally, she couldn't return to the subject, but
nothing, she realised with dismay on the homeward
journey, could distract her thoughts, blot out the
memory of his mouth on hers, its warmth, its deliberate
sensuality. Her anger still simmered, but with it brewed
another emotion, intangible as a subtle herb, but adding
an undoubted spice to his proximity, even though she sat
as far away as the confines of the limousine would allow.

'Philippa?' He broke in upon her thoughts, making
her start nervously, as though, in some way, he might
have read her mind. 'Do you think it would be possible
for you to hide your dislike of me—in front of your
sister, at least?'

She was tempted to repeat her accusation of hypocrisy. Naturally, he didn't want Mariana to suspect what
had passed between them.

'Why should I?' she challenged fiercely.

'Because it would distress her,' he said simply, which
seemed to confirm her conjecture.

'Very well, *senhor*,' she said scornfully, 'I shan't give
you away—this time.' She realised just what she had

said, its implications, at the identical moment that an
amused chuckle escaped him, but he did not take up the
advantage she'd given *him*. Instead, he remarked, 'A
case in point—you never address me as anything but
"*senhor*". It is scarcely . . .'

'That's the correct form of address,' she retorted. 'I'm
not totally ignorant of your customs.'

'*Sim*. It is perfectly correct—between polite strangers,
or mere acquaintances. But we are related and,' was he
actually teasing her? she wondered incredulously, 'we
are scarcely strangers—now? From now on, Philippa,
you will call me Carlos?'

'If I must,' she said ungraciously. 'But,' she stipu-
lated, 'only for Mariana's sake—not because I want to.'

The limousine drew to a halt at the steps of the Quinta
and Carlos turned in his seat, his eyes still amused, his
smile quizzical.

'For the present, I suppose that must suffice.' And his
lean fingers trailed a casual caress down the smoothness
of her cheek, leaving a tingling, strangely pleasurable
sensation in their wake. 'Some day,' his words halted her
as she was about to scramble from the car, 'if you wish it,
I will take you to Alcobaça and show you the tombs of
Pedro and Inez. There I will tell you their love story.'

'Th-thank you. I—I should like that,' she muttered, a
trifle incoherent as she hastened to escape.

But how did she really feel about his offer? she mused,
as she made her way up to her room. She would dearly
love to visit Alcobaça, of course, and the promise of a
story was an incentive. But her reactions to the idea of
Carlos's company were decidedly confusing.

She had detested him since their encounter at her
home. She *had* detested him, that was the operative

tense. But now? Now she was aware that her detestation had lessened, replaced by something far more irrational, an unwilling fascination. For she could no longer deny his attraction for her.

But that, she realised with relief, was only chemistry. You could acknowledge a man's physical attraction, without losing sight of the fact that his character was totally unlikeable. No, nothing had really changed. But all the same, she thought, the less she saw of her sister's future husband the better. Though, if Monty had his way, there would be many more outings. Just how long was that list he'd given Carlos?

She queried the point that evening, when she handed over her notes. After dinner, Monty had suddenly decided he wished to work. His brain, he said, was teeming with ideas.

But, as he skimmed over the sheets of paper she had covered with her neat handwriting, his face darkened and the pale yellow eyes looked up at her accusingly.

'What's all this?'

'The notes you wanted—the description of the Castelo dos Mouros and a little about its history.'

'But I didn't ask you to go there!' His lips tightened, always a preliminary to an outburst of choler. 'You're well aware, Pippa, history isn't my genre.' Suspiciously, 'You have handed me these by mistake, perhaps? Some private work which you've given precedence over mine?'

'No!' she said indignantly. 'The Castelo was the first place on the list Carlos had. You can't have forgotten?'

Monty fumbled in the waistcoat pocket of his evening suit, and drew out a crumpled piece of paper.

'This is my copy. See for yourself.'

The brief list was in Monty's own writing. Among the sites listed for her to visit, there was no mention whatsoever of the Castelo. What did it mean?

It meant, she realised in the same instant, that for some devious reason of his own, Carlos had lied to her. Why? The smooth brow above the grey eyes furrowed. She could only imagine one reason. If Monty were to become dissatisfied with her work, he might dismiss her. And if Monty sent her home, Carlos would be rid of her embarrassing presence.

'Well?' Monty didn't like to be kept waiting.

'I give you my word,' she met the pale eyes squarely, 'Carlos let me think our visit to the Castelo was your idea. May I keep this list? Then, in future, I can make certain I'm going where you want me to go.'

'Fortunately,' Monty said with heavy irony, 'my day was more fruitful.'

As the shorthand outlines flowed automatically from beneath her rapidly moving fingers, Pippa was able to take in its content. Monty had an unerring skill at portraying character. He prided himself on always drawing from life, on his skill in disguising the fact. And he took a malicious delight in bringing out the worst side of those who peopled his novels. This new work constituted an exceptionally brilliant exposé of a man and a woman, not yet in connected narrative—it was often Pippa's task to supply that—but in the form of two perfect descriptive cameos. By the end of the piece, she felt she knew them both as well as Monty certainly must.

The dictation ended, she gathered up her notebook, pens, and the notes on the Castelo.

'Leave those with me, dear girl,' Monty said casually. 'They may come in useful some time.'

Pippa didn't like to protest. The notes, though made in good faith, had been taken in time Monty was paying for. But if he didn't really want the information on the Castelo, she could have put it to good use. Still, she had a retentive memory and she could reproduce, almost verbatim, every word she'd written.

A pity, she brooded, as she made her way upstairs—Monty's apartments were on the ground floor out of consideration to his age—that it was now too late to confront Carlos, to face him with his deception. But he wasn't going to get away with it, and she felt a distinct sense of anticipation at the thought of tomorrow's inevitable confrontation.

But when tomorrow came, she was cheated of her thirst for conflict. Carlos, she learned, had gone out early. It was unlikely he would be back before evening.

'But I have promised to take Monty to Lisbon today,' Inez told her daughter helpfully. 'You could always come with us?'

'I'd love to,' Pippa said wistfully, thinking of the shops, the museums, the atmosphere of the city itself. But she knew what Monty's reaction would be to such a suggestion. 'No—I've got all last night's notes to type up.'

She saw her mother and Monty off in Inez's own limousine. Then, somewhat reluctantly, she returned to her room and the portable typewriter, which had formed part of her luggage.

As she typed, she gave occasional longing glances out of the window, grudging not only the sunshine and fresh air she was missing, but the day out she'd expected—for its valuable content, of course, *not* for Carlos's society.

Her work progressing more swiftly than she'd

supposed, she promised herself a walk after lunch.

For the first time in the two weeks she'd spent at the
Quinta, Pippa and Mariana sat alone together over a
meal—alone apart from the entrance and exit of dis-
creetly efficient servants. At first their conversation was
politely formal, until Pippa realised that Mariana was
not, as she had at first believed, hostile towards her, but
only painfully shy of the elder sister she could not
possibly have remembered.

Once Pippa discovered this, she began to draw
Mariana out, reminiscing about her own childhood in
Suffolk, describing for Mariana her life there, carefully
avoiding topics which Carlos might deem 'unsuitable'.
As a result, Mariana began to talk with increasing
spontaneity and confidence, though her English was
very stilted.

When Pippa told Mariana of her intention to take a
walk that afternoon, the younger girl brightened up still
more.

'May I come with you?' And as Pippa hesitated,
'Please! I am not allowed to walk unescorted, you
understand, but surely no one could object if I were with
you?'

Couldn't they, though? Pippa thought grimly. She
had a feeling that Carlos de Alvarez might just come up
with some objection, not least being her unsuitability as
a companion for her sister. But he was out for the day
and she had made such good progress with Mariana.

'All right,' she agreed. 'Where shall we go? You
choose. You know the area.'

At the top of a steep, unsurfaced lane, behind the

Quinta, lay the convent founded by Alfonso Henriques.
And it was in that direction that Mariana urged her elder
sister.

The ancient walls of the Convent of Santa Eulalia, its
well tended grounds, had a tranquil beauty that drew the
onlooker. But Pippa hadn't expected that they would
actually enter the convent precincts, much less the
building itself, and she was surprised by the ease with
which they gained admission.

'The nuns of Santa Eulalia are not an enclosed order,'
Mariana explained. 'I visit here often.'

Pippa had never been inside a convent, and for the
sake of curiosity if nothing else, she valued the
experience. Its interior was simple, in keeping with the
nuns' vows of poverty. But even the simplest item
gleamed with evidence of their devoted care. Only the
private chapel was ornate, with its intricately carved
choir stalls, gilded grillework, fine paintings, and of
course, the statues—statues everywhere.

Another surprise to Pippa was the great affection with
which the nuns greeted Mariana, a warmth which
extended itself to her sister, even though Pippa could not
understand the torrent of Portuguese that enveloped
her.

Only the Superior, Soror Maria Onofrio, spoke a little
English, and in her austere tiny parlour, she astonished
Pippa by talking of her hopes for Mariana.

'Your sister, Senhorita Lang, has a true vocation. She
wishes much to join us here, and I understand that with
your help this will indeed be possible.' Her homely face
crumpled into a beaming smile as she regarded the
astonished girl.

Pippa turned to her sister, who had sat, eyes modestly

downcast during the Superior's eulogies.

'Mariana, is this true? You really want to become a nun? I thought you were to marry C...?'

'*Não!*' Mariana said with great conviction. 'I shall never marry. More than anything else in the world, I wish to join the sisterhood here.'

Pippa couldn't understand her sister's desire for the religious life, but supposed it must be due to the upbringing Mariana had received since Inez had brought the younger girl home to Portugal.

'Well, it's your life,' she said at last.

'Then you *will* help?' Mariana's normal serenity, which Pippa had at first taken for sulky hostility, had been replaced by an unusual animation.

'I don't see what I can do,' she objected. 'If it's a question of breaking it to *Mãe*, you must know better than I what her reaction will be.'

But Mariana's request was so unexpected that Pippa was rendered temporarily speechless.

'You are the only one who *can* help me—by marrying Cousin Carlos!'

CHAPTER FIVE

'YOU'VE got to be joking!' Pippa repeated her incredulous exclamation, as she and Mariana left the convent and retraced their steps in the direction of the Quinta de Estrella, whose rooftops shining in the late afternoon sunlight could just be seen far below them.

'No.' Mariana sounded genuinely puzzled. 'I do not joke. Why should I? To me it is a matter of great seriousness, that I should be allowed to follow my vocation.'

'I meant about *me* marrying Carlos. Even if I were willing—which I'm not—he wouldn't touch me with a ...' She stopped short, remembering she mustn't allude to the reasons for Carlos's disapproval of her.

'There is someone else?' Mariana asked anxiously. 'You are already betrothed? Perhaps to Senhor Makin?'

'No!' Pippa said. 'Like you, I don't want to marry anyone.'

'You have the vocation too? But I thought ...'

Pippa laughed at her surprised intonation.

'Can you see *me* as a nun?' Then she sobered, realising that to Mariana it was no joke. 'No, I've no religious inclinations, but something similar, I suppose. I want a career. I want to be a writer, and Monty says that to be a successful one you need to be single-minded, selfish even—that a writer hasn't time for anyone else.'

Mariana halted, her smooth features puckered in distress as she looked up at her taller sister.

'But nor do I wish to marry. That is how *I* feel. I have

no time for anyone but God. Yet one of us must marry
Carlos, for *Mãe's* sake.'

Pippa too stood still, her grey eyes stormy as she
surveyed her sister's troubled face.

'That's ridiculous! Look, Mariana,' she said firmly.
'The days when people could be forced into marriage are
long past. I won't be blackmailed and neither should you
be. If you really want to become a nun, neither *Mãe* nor
Carlos can stop you—and I can't believe he'd really
throw *Mãe* out. Even he couldn't be that inhuman.'

'Carlos? Inhuman?' Mariana was shocked. 'You
think that of him? Oh no, he has always been kindness
itself to me.'

'Naturally! Because he expects you to marry him. You
watch him change when you tell him ...'

'Carlos already knows my wishes ...'

'You've told him? When?'

'Before he left for England this last time.'

Carlos had known—*before* he'd visited Little Pennyfeather. He couldn't possibly have come there to look *her*
over, could he? As the only other candidate for his
hand? Pippa quailed. How cold-blooded it sounded.
And yet, *was* Carlos cold-blooded?

Her cheeks ran fiery colour as she remembered the
warmth, the sensuality of his kiss. No, Carlos was not a
passionless man, far from it. And if he could kiss her like
that, when he didn't even approve of her, how would it
be if he were in love? Best not to imagine such things,
she decided hastily.

'And *Mãe?*' she asked Mariana. 'Does she know?
Does she approve?'

'She knows, but,' Mariana's downcast face was
unhappy, 'she will only give her consent, release the

dowry I need, if *you* marry Carlos. Otherwise, she says *I*
must!'

'I don't believe it!' Pippa was not doubting Mariana's
word, only the notion that Inez could be so unscrupulous. 'She couldn't be that hard-hearted!' she exclaimed.
But could she? Hadn't Inez shown considerable ruth-
lessness in leaving husband, home and one of her
daughters? And for what reason? Pippa still didn't
know.

'But it is true,' Mariana asserted. 'Not that she wishes
to be unkind to me, I'm sure. But she will do anything—
anything to remain at the Quinta, she has told me this.
And she *will* withhold the dowry that a nun must take
with her when she enters the order.'

'Why on earth is *Mãe* so desperate to stay at the
Quinta? If she has money, why can't she buy her own
place?'

'She has no money of her own—only the annual
interest on that left in trust by our grandfather—for us,
when we marry. He disapproved of *Mãe's* marriage to
our father. Besides, it would not be considered suitable
here for a woman of good social standing to live alone.
She must live under the protection of a male relative.' It
was the longest speech Pippa had ever heard Mariana
make.

'But if you go into the convent, you won't *be* getting
married, so ...?'

'It is the same thing. I shall become a Bride of Christ,'
Mariana said with quiet pride. 'And Carlos says that is
sufficient entitlement for me to receive my inheritance.'

'But *why* is it so important to *Mãe* to stay on here?'
Pippa puzzled again. 'Surely, after all the years she spent
in England, she doesn't go along with all this male
dominance?'

To her amazement, Pippa saw that Mariana was blushing.

'It is not for me to tell. I am not even supposed to know. I found out only by accident.'

'Mariana,' Pippa coaxed. 'I'm your sister. Surely it wouldn't be wrong to tell me—especially since it seems to affect us both?'

After a few doubtful sideways glances and more blushing, Mariana seemed to take courage.

'*Sim*. Perhaps you are right. It is a secret I have not enjoyed knowing. Once I have told you, perhaps I can forget about it.'

One by one, Mariana began to pluck the glossy leaves from one of the bougainvillaeas that lined their path, her eyes intent upon her task, as though she could not meet Pippa's intent gaze.

'I overheard *Mãe* talking with Senhor Mortimer. I did not mean to eavesdrop, but what she said interested me, so . . .' She sighed. 'It is a sin, no, curiosity? I shall have to confess it.'

Pippa checked a protest. She didn't want Mariana to stop now.

'*Mãe* spoke of the days when she was young—about my age. She was in love. I do not know with whom. She did not speak his name, but it was not possible for her to marry this man—again I do not know why. But there was a great quarrel between her and our Grandfather de Alvarez. It was then she met *Pai*. He was a student then—on a walking tour with friends. He fell in love with her. She met him secretly and in the end ran away with him.'

'Goodness! How romantic!' Pippa couldn't restrain the comment. 'Imagine Dad doing such a thing.'

'No—not romantic,' Mariana disagreed sadly, 'for

she was not in love with *Pai*. It was an act of defiance.
She told Senhor Mortimer that she had often regretted
it—if she had not had us to love——' Mariana shrugged.
'But then, thirteen years ago, she learned something
that made her determined to return to Sintra, to be near
the man she loved.'

'Learned what?' Pippa was agog.

'I do not know,' Mariana confessed. 'That was when I
realised I should not be listening and so I went away.'

Pippa could have screamed with frustration. To have
come so near to the answer to a question that had always
plagued her. Wild speculation ran rife in Pippa's mind,
keeping her silent for the remainder of their walk. Who
was the man the young Inez de Alvarez had loved? A
thought struck her. It couldn't have been—Carlos? For
one thing she must be seven or eight years older than he.
Although these days, she mused, that didn't seem to
matter so much.

But no. That was ridiculous. If *Mãe* were in love with
Carlos, she wouldn't be encouraging him to marry one
of her daughters; and Carlos's principles were too rigid,
weren't they, to countenance any relationship with a
married woman?

Yet she couldn't be certain. After all, what did she
really know of Carlos de Alvarez? He could have lied to
her about his moral standards. An arrogant man, he
might not apply to himself the standards he expected of
others.

At the steps of the Quinta, Mariana touched her
sister's arm.

'What have you decided, Pippa?'

Decided? Until that moment Pippa had reached no
conclusions, but now, suddenly, it came to her what she
must do.

'I shall speak to Carlos, of course.'

'Oh!' Mariana breathed. 'Thank you, Pippa, thank you. But—but wouldn't it be more—more suitable if you waited for *him* to speak to you?'

Pippa stared at her in amusement. Did the silly goose really think she intended proposing to the man? Nothing could be further from her intentions. On the point of saying so, she bit back the words. No need to worry Mariana with the truth. She was, Pippa realised with wry amusement, falling into the family custom of avoiding any upset to her sister. But it was an attitude she could now understand, in view of Mariana's proven unworldliness.

'It might be more suitable in Portuguese eyes, but I've been brought up in England. I'm used to speaking my mind—and, frankly, I'd just as soon have the whole thing over and done with.'

Mariana inclined her head, as if she could at least understand this point of view and no more was said between them on the subject.

As she dressed for dinner that evening, Pippa considered how best to broach the subject uppermost in her mind. It would mean confronting Carlos on his own, not a prospect she relished. But she didn't want any witnesses to what she intended to say. After dinner, she would request a private interview with him.

Inez and Monty had still not returned from Lisbon, when the grandfather clock in the tiled hallway struck eight, and when Pippa entered the *sala*, it was to find Carlos its sole occupant. She hesitated on the threshold. She hadn't expected to be alone with him so soon, had not steadied herself for the encounter.

With concealed amusement, Carlos watched Pippa's

entrance. She had taken great pains with her appearance tonight, and he thought he knew why.

She had done what many women with her colouring would not have dared to do, worn pink, but it was such a subtle shade that with every movement of her long, graceful bódy the material seemed to shimmer towards greys and violets. The dress, he found himself noting appraisingly, moulded and emphasised her high, full breasts, hugged the trim waist, shifted caressingly to the sway of her hips. The material would be soft, silky to the touch. As she came closer, a subtle floral perfume assured his nostrils of what his eyes already perceived, her flawless femininity.

'Come in, Philippa. As you see, we dine alone tonight, you and I.' For some reason his voice sounded unusually husky, and nervously, Pippa edged the tip of her tongue over suddenly dry lips.

'My—my mother? Monty?'

'Staying overnight at the apartment in Lisbon. Senhor Mortimer found his day tiring.'

'And—Mariana?' Mariana's presence, though not obtrusive, would have at least defused the explosive tension Pippa had felt from the moment she'd walked into the room—and it wasn't just her own nervousness at the thought of what she intended to say to him.

'Dining in her own room, at her own request.'

'She's—not well?' Pippa forgot nerves in concern.

'Quite well. Considerately, she suggested that we might speak more freely without her.' He moved suddenly towards Pippa and almost she flinched away, until she realised his purpose was merely to offer her his arm. 'Shall we go in? Dinner is about to be served.'

It was ridiculous how cold, how tremulous her fingers felt as she placed them on the proffered arm. The fine

material of his sleeve couldn't disguise the muscular
hardness it concealed, or the warmth of his body; and
when he covered her hand with his free one, it was as
though an electric current coursed through her, making
the blood race in her veins, the throb of her heart almost
deafening her.

Although they were dining tête-à-tête, none of the
formalities had been spared. The table was laid as
elaborately as usual, and Pippa viewed apprehensively
the prospect of tackling several courses, with what she
proposed to say to him lying sickly on her stomach. Yet
good manners decreed she wait until they had eaten to
confront him.

Carlos drew out her chair, and his proximity as she sat
sent shudders down her spine, but whether of fear or
excitement she could not tell, for she felt both in equal
measure.

Sternly, she reminded herself that physically attractive he might be, but likeable he was not. Any man who
could stoop to emotional blackmail to gain such paltry
ends . . . She couldn't see what was so special about being
a de Alvarez.

'You have something you wish to say to me.' Carlos
seemed less concerned with the niceties of behaviour
than she, but how did he know? Was there something
about her expression, her manner, that betrayed her
desire to take issue with him?

'So,' he went on, 'you are eager to become my wife?'

'What? *What* did you say?' Pippa had heard him
perfectly well, but the total unexpectedness of his words
put her at a loss for a coherent rejoinder. A spoonful of
soup poised half-way to her lips, she stared as if
mesmerized into azure blue eyes.

'I thought I had expressed myself quite clearly. I said,

you wish to marry me?'

'I most certainly don't. Whatever gave you that idea?' Then she groaned, 'O Lord, Mariana! She ...'

'*Sim.* Mariana warned me of your intention to propose. Unusual, but then English customs are different. Thoughtful child that she is, she felt it would spare you embarrassment if I knew of your willingness and spoke first.'

Carefully, because her hand was shaking so much, Pippa returned the heavy silver spoon to her dish. She took pains with her enunciation of the words that seemed to come with difficulty.

'Mariana misunderstood. When I told her I was going to speak to you, I meant I intended to tell you just what I think of the—emotional blackmail you're exerting on her, on my mother ...'

'Blackmail!' Carlos too had ceased to eat and the black bar of his brows came down over the bridge of his perfectly chiselled nose. 'What is this you are saying? Of what heinous crime are you daring to accuse me?'

'Blackmail!' she repeated hardily. 'You understand the meaning of the word, I suppose?'

'*Sim!* I understand!' He pushed back his chair and rose, advancing towards her. 'And I demand an explanation of this outrageous ...'

'Don't worry!' Pippa was standing too now, outwardly courageous, inwardly poised for flight. 'You're going to get your explanation. Put succinctly, it's this. According to my mother, if you don't get to marry one of her daughters, you'll throw her out.'

'That is quite ...'

'Wait! I haven't finished. And because of this, *Mãe* in turn is refusing to give Mariana the dowry she needs as a nun—because if I won't marry you—and I most certainly won't—Mariana must. What's that if not blackmail?' she demanded, tilting her chin at him.

During her impassioned speech, she had felt her lips begin to quiver uncontrollably and now she pressed them together. She must not destroy the effect of her defiance by bursting into tears. Why she felt tearful she couldn't think. Anger didn't usually affect her this way.

The answer she demanded was not immediately forthcoming. Instead, she found her arm taken in a none too gentle grip, as Carlos marched her out of the dining-room, past a string of bewildered servants and into the library.

'Your dinner?' she ventured.

'You,' he informed her grimly, 'have just taken away every vestige of my appetite—and you do not eat either, until we have this matter resolved.'

Right now the very thought of food made her stomach churn. In fact, she wondered if she'd ever be able to eat under Carlos's roof again. The muscles of her throat seemed constricted in a kind of paralysis that surely would prevent her swallowing.

Unceremoniously, he thrust her into one of the large leather chairs, while he himself restlessly paced the room, his features drawn into grim lines. As the silence lengthened, so Pippa's tension increased. And though she dreaded what he would say or do, she had reached the point where she felt any outcome would be better than its anticipation.

Finally, he turned to look at her but to her relief, this time he kept his distance. It was difficult to think coolly, logically when he was near her.

'We will deal with the case of Mariana first since that is the easiest, the least complicated. I was not aware that Inez was holding over her head the matter of her dowry.

But if *Mariana* says it is so, I have no reason to doubt it. Mariana never lies.'

Was he implying that she, Pippa, *did* lie? It was no use. She couldn't sit still under his glittering gaze. She rose to her feet.

'Mariana *did* say that.'

'Then I must speak to Inez. In the event of her proving intractable, I shall myself provide Mariana's dowry.'

Pippa stared at him, then, slowly, 'She said you understood. But,' doubtfully, 'you really don't mind, if she enters the convent?'

'Certainly not. It is a matter of pride for a family to have a relative enter a religious order.'

Pippa shrugged, still unwilling to believe in his altruism.

'What about my mother, then? You surely don't accuse her of lying?'

'Of lying?' He considered the word. 'Perhaps not directly, but of practising deception for her own ends, certainly. Inez has her own peculiar brand of morality—if she wishes a thing to be, then it is so. I did not approve of her wilful desertion of your father, but she knows I would never see a member of my family homeless.'

'Then why...?' Pippa stopped. It was too embarrassing.

'Why is she so eager to see me married to one of her daughters?' Suddenly, he smiled and the effect was astonishing, sunshine after storm. 'And in the circumstances, to you?'

Pippa nodded, feeling unaccountably, painfully shy. Right at this moment, he did not seem at all fearsome. He was speaking quietly, thoughtfully, and one by one he was disposing of her reasons for disliking him—of all her reasons but one, she reminded herself, hardening her heart against the charm that, insidiously, was fighting her resolve to dislike, to distrust him.

'If I *were* to marry again . . .'

'Again!' Pippa felt herself go rigid with shock. 'You—you've been married before?'

'*Sim!*' His voice was suddenly harsh. 'I am a widower. But you need not concern yourself with that—as I was about to say—*if* I married outside the family—as I had recently considered doing—it is conceivable that my wife might not wish to have a relative, and a female one at that, under the same roof.'

'You—you've considered marrying—s-someone else?' Illogical pain tore at Pippa's heart.

'*Sim.* I have been a widower these thirteen years. I have sometimes considered that the Quinta should have a mistress other than your mother.'

Who had Carlos considered marrying? Was there still a chance that he might settle on this other, unknown woman? But he was speaking again.

'In that case, I should be forced to make other arrangements for Inez—perhaps giving her permanent use of the Lisbon apartment—which would not suit her convenience at all. However, if my wife were also Inez's daughter, there might not be the same objection. You see the reasons behind her machinations? Believe me, Inez has very strong reason for wishing to stay in this area. Which is . . .'

'She wants to be in Sintra to be near the man she loves.' Though her mind was still in a whirl of conjecture concerning Carlos's previous marriage, and the knowledge that he had been contemplating taking a wife *before* she had come to Portugal, Pippa had wit enough left to discover the clue for herself. '*He* lives in

Sintra, doesn't he? And I thought ...' She cut short what she'd been about to say.

'Yes?'

'I thought perhaps that man was you, but ...'

Carlos threw back his head in a great shout of laughter. Pippa had never seen him so uninhibited, as he was in this paroxysm of genuine amusement. In laughter he looked younger, infinitely more approachable—and—she had to admit it—even more compellingly attractive than usual.

'But,' she went on, with great dignity, when he had sobered once more, 'I realised it was impossible—at least, when she was eighteen it would have been. You would have been only ...'

'Thirteen,' he confirmed. 'Yes.'

'Though I suppose,' she went on thoughtfully, 'that age difference wouldn't matter so much now.'

'And would it matter to you, Philippa, if your mother and I were in love?'

'I—no, of course—yes ...' She stumbled, then endeavoured to explain the contradictory words. 'No, it wouldn't matter—not on my own account.' Why should it, she asked herself doubtfully. 'But my father—she's still married to him. I ...'

'It really wouldn't matter to you personally?' He moved slowly, deliberately, towards her and she backed away until she could retreat no further. He didn't touch her but stood looking down at her, his expression unreadable.

'N-no!'

'You really hadn't decided to marry me? To sacrifice yourself for your mother and sister?'

'Certainly not!' she was able to reply with great positiveness.

'You disappoint me!' Was that a gleam of amusement in his eyes?

'I'd never marry for a reason like that. And if you ever thought so—any of you . . .'

'For what reason *would* you marry, Philippa?' Words and eyes probed.

'Only—only in the very unlikely event of my falling in love,' she told him, trying unsuccessfully to avoid his gaze, wishing he would move and let her escape from the angle of the bookshelves where he had cornered her.

'Why so unlikely?'

'Because I'm determined not to fall in love,' she said fiercely. 'I want to be independent. I want to run my own life, to be beholden to no one. I want to make a name for myself—my own name—as a writer.'

'I see,' He said it consideringly. 'You realise, of course, that you will never do so, not while you work for Senhor Mortimer?'

'Of course I will. Monty's taught me all I know.'

'Hmm,' was his irritating enigmatic reply. Then, 'And what will you do, if some day, despite yourself, you fall helplessly in love? Will you deny yourself—and the man—for the sake of a few paltry books?'

'Books outlive people,' she retorted.

'That rather depends upon the author. Are you really convinced you have it in you to become another Dickens? A Monteiro? What a pity if you should find your life spent to no avail. What if life's greatest purpose for a woman should remain unfulfilled for nothing gained?'

'By that, I suppose, you mean being at a man's beck and call!'

'Philippa! Philippa!' He raised his hands as if in despair, and she couldn't be sure it was only accidental—

a fingertip brushed her breast, eliciting a sensation
fleetingly exquisite. 'Where do you get your ideas?' he
mocked. 'A man does not look for a servant when he
marries. He looks for someone to fill his heart . . .'

'And his bed?' she snapped, because her nerves were
getting the better of her and because that exquisite
sensastion had been too brief for memory to encapsulate,
to analyse.

'I have told you before—do not generalise. Physical
love between man and woman is important—of course it
is. But please credit some men at least with the ability to
recognise other prerequisites.'

'Such as?' Pippa took refuge in sarcasm from the
strange sensations gripping her. 'Cooking . . .?'

The finger that lifted her chin was strong. And it
lingered—almost—caressingly.

'You have a short memory, my . . . I thought we had
already discounted the role of servant? The woman I
shall marry . . .' He paused thoughtfully.

How had they got on to this subject? It was one Pippa
didn't want to pursue. She didn't want to know Carlos
de Alvarez's requirements of a woman. She was afraid of
knowing them!

'The woman I shall marry,' he went on slowly, his
eyes still on her face, '*if* I remarry, that is, shall be so
closely allied to me mentally and spiritually, that we
shall be as one even before we come together in the
marriage bed.'

Unexpectedly, Pippa found herself trembling. There
was something in the mellow intonation, the sincerity
behind the softly spoken words that touched an
answering chord, some unguessed core of feeling within
her.

Desperately, she sought for a change of subject. He

was coming too close to her, not only physically, but in a growing empathy that threatened her independence of spirit.

But her brain was functioning too slowly for effective evasion. The caressing finger had moved from her chin to her jaw-line, his whole hand to the nape of her neck, cupping it with a possessiveness which sent waves of excited fear rippling along her spine.

The elusive scent of aftershave assailed her nostrils and then, he brought both hands into play, sliding them over her shoulders, easing her up against the hardness of his body, fastening on her hips, urging her quivering figure closer still, making her shudderingly aware of his maleness.

He was going to kiss her, she panicked, and there wasn't a thing she was capable of doing about it. The rise and fall of his chest against her breasts brought its own peculiar excitement, an involuntary response she could not control. She knew that, beneath the silky fabric of her dress, her nipples would be taut; they ached for his touch.

'Carlos!'

She was not aware that she had even murmured his name aloud, but her parted lips gave him the access he sought to the moistness of her mouth, his jerky breathing mingling with hers.

His kiss had a hard urgency that incited a hitherto unsuspected sensuality deep inside her. She tried to fight the insidious unwanted desire coiling within her. But somehow her trembling hands had reached his shoulders. Then her arms were around his neck, her fingers burying themselves frantically in the thick dark hair. His kiss deepened, a sensual exploration of the inner softness of her mouth. She felt faint, disorientated.

What was she doing, a corner of her mind demanded, allowing Carlos de Alvarez to make love to her like this? He didn't like her, she didn't like him, yet she was ardently, passionately responding to him, and the realisation frightened her.

'Carlos!' she said again, but this time it was a cry for mercy.

For an instant, he raised his head and she saw the expression on his face, the flare of the aristocratic nostrils, the dark, glittering intensity of his eyes, before his lips claimed hers again and she fell once more under the powerful hypnotism of his kisses.

Unaware of the provocation she offered him, she moved erotically against him, heard the low growl in his throat. His hand caressed her breasts, an experienced and practised exploration, moulding them with an urgent hunger, making her incapable of any coherent thought. But as his fingers moved to invade the deep V of her neckline, warning bells jangled in her bemused brain.

She didn't want Carlos de Alvarez to make love to her; she didn't want any man. She wanted to remain free— free from the weakness of a need that would threaten her ability to direct her own life, and with the flash of sanity came the memory of further questions she'd wanted to ask him. She pushed the intrusive hands away, wrenched her lips from his.

'Carlos! No! Stop. I mean it! Let me go!'

His dark eyes were still alight with passion, his breathing still ragged. She could feel the tenseness of his frustration, and she sought for words that would penetrate beyond the physical to his sense of propriety.

'Would you treat a Portuguese girl like this?'

For a moment she thought she hadn't got through to

him. Then he relaxed, moved away from her, cleared his throat huskily.

'You're right, of course. I apologise. I'm afraid our conversation seemed to lead naturally to ...'

'But we hadn't *finished* our conversation.' With nervous hands she smoothed down her dress. Though he had released her, she did not immediately leave the support of the shelves against which she leant. 'You didn't tell me—who is the man my mother loves?'

'That's not for me to tell you—not without Inez's permission.' He turned to face her and she saw that he at least was now in control of himself, his features once more composed and expressionless. 'And now—you have been most assiduous in your questioning of me—I feel entitled to reciprocate. Six years ago—I prevented you from taking your own life. Tell me—you never felt any inclination to do so again?'

'To take my own life?' What ailed the man? 'I've never, never had any such intention!'

'Yet you threw yourself into the river,' he accused. 'You ...'

'I *fell* into the river. It was an accident.'

'You—fell?' He sounded disbelieving. 'Yet you resented my help.'

'Of course I did,' Pippa said scornfully. She didn't know quite whether to be angry or amused, but at least the tension had gone out of the atmosphere. 'I've lived all my life near that river. I know every inch of it. I wasn't in any danger. If you hadn't come along, I'd have been perfectly all right.'

'But,' perplexity still corrugated his handsome face, 'your pregnancy. You were disturbed—afraid ...'

'Senhor de Alvarez!' She said his name coldly, deliberately formal, because in his arms she'd said his first name with too much feeling. 'Whatever I am, I'm not a coward. I wouldn't dream of taking my own life.'

'So, I misunderstood. I apologise,' he said stiffly, then with a disconcerting softening of his manner, 'And I am glad, Philippa, that . . .'

'That I've no tendencies that way?' she said, deliberately flippant, because she was afraid of what he might be going to say. 'Yes, I suppose a suicide in the family would be embarrassing.'

'You are determined to quarrel with me, Philippa.' He sounded faintly regretful. 'I do not know why, but,' he shrugged, 'so be it. And since you are already angry with me, I will venture to ask about your child.'

'The—the child?'

'*Sim*. I should like to know about the child.'

'Because he would have a drop of de Alvarez blood? But surely, *senhor*, it would be much too diluted to warrant your interest?'

'So!' he breathed. Surely that wasn't satisfaction she detected? 'There is a child. You did not have an abortion.'

Aghast, Pippa stared at him.

'No, I did not!' she told him from between clenched teeth. 'I'd no more take my child's life than I would my own. What an opinion you must have of me. How could you bear to touch me? How relieved you must be . . .'

'Relieved? Yes, I am relieved, but it is because you are not as I feared. The mistake you made in your youthful ignorance is forgivable, but . . .'

'Forgivable!' Pippa's voice rose an octave. 'Who the hell do you think you are to speak of forgiveness? God? I don't want or need *your* forgiveness for anything I've ever done in my life. Goodnight, *senhor*. For obvious reasons, I'll try to keep out of your way for as long as

Monty insists on staying under your roof. But believe me, he can't leave here soon enough.'

Why, why, why didn't you tell him? she stormed at her tear-stained reflection in the bedroom mirror. Why didn't you tell him there was no pregnancy, no baby? Why? Because, her reflection told her, you couldn't have borne any more of his—his arrogant 'relief'—his 'forgiveness'—as if you were a reclaimed black sheep.

And—she told herself in a calmer moment, later, much much later, after the storm of tears had abated into cold, dreary sanity—because you didn't want to hear him say you were, after all, fit to be his wife, the mother of future de Alvarezes. Because you wouldn't want that admission on those terms—but because he loved you. And how was it possible, she wondered incredulously, to feel jealousy of a dead woman—because *she* had, presumably, known Carlos's love; and what about this other woman he had considered marrying . . .?

Damn, damn, damn it all to hell! And damn him! In lieu of anything, or anyone else, Pippa punched her crumpled pillow. I must be out of my tiny mind!

But it wasn't her mind that was at fault, she knew. It was her stupid, rebellious heart that had gone astray, played the traitor, plunging her, before intellect could restrain its waywardness, fathoms deep into love with a man who had believed her capable of unspeakable things.

CHAPTER SIX

'*Bom dia*, Philippa. I have been planning today's itinerary.'

Pippa looked at Carlos in disbelief, and met only a smiling, ingenuous gaze. She'd had to steel herself to come down to breakfast this morning, had in fact left it as late as possible, in the hope that he would have eaten and gone out. He couldn't possibly have forgotten last night's declaration of intent to avoid him?

'You had not forgotten Senhor Mortimer's list?' he asked.

No, she hadn't, but she had hoped he might have done, so that in future, she might be allowed to tackle her assignment unsupervised.

'His list or *your* version of it?' she enquired tartly but Carlos was cheerfully unperturbed by her caustic manner.

'So! My sins have found me out! But I wanted you to know something of the scenes of our family's proud history—our connection with the kings of Portugal— and you must admit, Philippa, that you enjoyed the Castelo dos Mouros.' A reminiscently sensual smile accompanied the light, mocking tone.

She couldn't deny it, any more than she could forget that it was at the Castelo that Carlos had first kissed her, and she felt the responsive colour rising in her cheeks.

'Maybe I did,' she said hastily, 'but Monty was furious and I don't blame him. He's not paying me to . . .'

'I promise you, Philippa, in future we will adhere most religiously to the *senhor's* list of ...'

'You mean *I* will,' Pippa interrupted, 'I'd rather do my work without ...'

'Without me to—"distract" *was* the word you used?' He was gently laughing at her and, while it annoyed, Pippa had to marvel at how much he had mellowed in the past day or two. It was, she discovered, since Peter had left. Or was that just coincidence?

Carlos leant across the width of the table, recalling her wandering attention with the touch of his hand on hers, and she felt no compulsion to draw away.

'If I give you my promise, Philippa, that there will be no more "distractions", will you permit that I escort you, assist you with your research work?'

She swallowed, as oddly reluctant to refuse his softly spoken request as earlier she had been reluctant to accept his company.

'I—I ...'

'*Por favor!*' he coaxed.

Why had she given in without further protest? But she wasn't sorry. The late summer day was a glorious one, the scenery they traversed magnificent, and Carlos's company enhanced the whole.

Between Sintra and the coast, a winding road ran through damp, cool, silent forests, the air smelling strongly of moss and wet bark, and Pippa exclaimed appreciatively.

'You are coming to love this country, I believe,' Carlos said perceptively. 'But beware, Philippa. Sintra exerts a spell from which there is no release.'

She could well believe it. But it was not Sintra alone that was beginning to enslave her.

'Carlos,' she asked curiously, 'don't you have to—to work?'

He angled an amused glance at her.

'Not in the sense you mean—to earn a living. I fear I am disgustingly rich—not through any merits of my own, but through inheritance. Do you find that shocking?'

'No,' she said thoughtfully. 'After all, you couldn't help inheriting. But what *is* important,' and censure crept into her tone, 'is the use you make of your money. Even if people are rich, I believe they should still do something—for the sake of their own self-respect—and certainly for the good of others.'

He didn't answer and she wondered a little anxiously if she had offended him, but he was pointing ahead of them.

'The sea!'

The road here was lined with summer houses, half hidden in pinewoods, that grew down to the sands of Praia das Macas, a beach, Carlos told her, which was much frequented in the holiday season.

'For myself, I prefer Azenhas do Mar. You will see why, I think.'

He drove on, past Praia Grande, its sand dunes and thundering breakers, to where the coastline grew wilder still, pitted with coves torn out of the land by great Atlantic rollers. Villages of unspoilt, colour-washed houses perched on high ledges of rock where only cistus and heathers had survived the long, torrid months of sunshine. Far below them, Pippa could see the mill-ponds that gave the place its name, washed by the waves of the incoming sea.

All too soon for her, Carlos turned the limousine

inland again, back through the pinewoods and into vine-growing country.

Just beyond Colares they turned off the road, through a stone gateway, along a driveway that bisected a leafy park. Pippa caught her breath as the house and its box-edged gardens came into sight.

'Beautiful, is it not?' Carlos agreed. 'Sixteenth century—the Casa do Sol. Home of my friend Felipe Monteiro,' he paused, then, 'the brother of Carmela, my late wife.'

Startled, Pippa shot a sideways glance at him. Why on earth had he brought her here? But his expression was inscrutable as he drew her attention to the finer points of the house's architecture.

It was, indeed, beautiful, a white, two-storied building, its corners adorned with cantaloupe-melon cupolas, but in Pippa's eyes it could not outrank the Quinta de Estrella. Beyond the house rose a strange science-fiction scene, an area of white domes—the winery, Carlos explained, where a delicious red wine, famous for centuries, was still produced.

'Senhor Monteiro is a winegrower?'

'*Sim*. Although these days he is forced to leave everything to his overseer.' And, as Pippa looked questioningly, 'You will see for yourself.'

The rooms of the Casa do Sol were full of priceless antique furnishings and paintings. Sunlight reflected off highly polished brass, and green houseplants abounded, all showing every evidence of loving care.

A manservant showed them into the main *sala*, where a middle-aged woman bent over a tapestry frame, working an intricate design in glowing colours. As they entered, she turned, a smile of pleasure irradiating her features—but such homely features, sallow and un-

adorned, her sparse grey hair drawn back in a severe
knot, unremarkable eyes framed by metal spectacles.
What a contrast, Pippa thought, with the richness and
beauty of her surroundings, her exquisite craftwork.

But Carlos bent over her hand as if she were an
acknowledged beauty.

'Luisa!'

'Carlos!' A rapid spate of words indicated her pleasure
at seeing him, but when Carlos, introducing Pippa,
explained that she spoke no Portuguese, Luisa Monteiro
repeated her greeting for Pippa's benefit.

'You are most welcome. Felipe will be delighted. We
receive so few visitors. Sit down, sit down! You will take
a glass of our own good wine?'

Luisa Monteiro was entirely unlike Pippa's conception of a Portuguese woman—energetic, bustling, rapid
of speech, she was a total contrast to the languidness of
Inez de Alvarez, Pippa's only real point of comparison.

Servants were sent hurrying in search of Don Felipe,
while others fetched wine, and all the time, in between
issuing rapid directions, Luisa Monteiro quizzed Carlos
about his recent visit to England.

'You were reluctant to go, *sim*? But all has turned out
well?' Her smiling gaze embraced a bewildered Pippa.

She questioned Pippa, too, about her opinion of
Portugal, showed interest in her work for Monty, and it
was only when Inez's name was mentioned that Pippa
detected a slight cooling in the atmosphere of welcome.

'You certainly do not take after her, but perhaps that
is ...'

'Carlos, my good friend!' Whatever Luisa had been
going to say was interrupted by the arrival of Felipe
Monteiro—in a self-propelled wheelchair. 'And you
have brought us a visitor—and such a charming one—as

is her dear mother.'

Well, he seemed to like Inez all right. But then Pippa
had sometimes found that plain women disliked beautiful ones and resented the admiration of their menfolk.

The Monteiros were not as fluent in their English as
Carlos, and when, from time to time, inevitably, they
reverted to their own language, Pippa took the opportunity to study the oddly assorted pair.

Luisa and Felipe made an interesting contrast, she so
plain, he so very handsome. Had his sister, Carlos's
wife—her heart contracted painfully at the thought—
been as beautiful as her brother was handsome? Felipe
must have been even more so before whatever affliction
had confined him to a wheelchair sprinkled grey the
dark hair and lined the face with pain. But he could
never have been half as attractive as Carlos, she found
herself thinking, and glanced towards him to confirm
this impression. To her confusion, she found his blue
eyes on her, and she knew his quizzical smile was for the
colour that suffused her cheeks.

The more she watched and listened to the Monteiros,
as they spoke in a mixture of languages, apologising
continually to her for their lapses, the greater grew
Pippa's sense of familiarity, of déjà vu.

Then, it came to her. Monty's character studies!
Undoubtedly, these were the models for those two
perfect cameos of insight. So she was nothing loath when
the Monteiros invited them to stay to lunch. The couple
interested her intensely; Monty would undoubtedly ask
her for her impressions. When, after lunch, Felipe
carried Carlos off to inspect a revolutionary new wine
press he'd recently acquired, Pippa was more than
happy to sit and watch Luisa at her tapestry and listen.

'They are good friends,' Luisa said fondly, 'despite

the difference in their ages. Felipe likes to play as active a part as possible in the running of the wine house. He has had special ramps constructed for his wheelchair, so that he may have easy access to any of the processes.'

'How did he ...? Was it ...?' Pippa enquired delicately.

'A motoring accident—thirteen years ago—*ai*, how time goes by! His wife, Maria, his children, our beloved Carmela, too—all were fatally injured, but Felipe survived as you see him.'

'His wife!' Pippa exclaimed. 'But I thought you ...?

'*Não! Não!*' Luisa laughed with easy self-deprecation. 'What would a handsome man like Felipe do with a wife such as I?' It was obvious that she adored him. 'He is my big brother. I have never married—for obvious reasons!' Again, that wry self-mockery. 'Felipe and Carmela were the beautiful ones. And it is just as well I never married, for now Felipe is all my care.'

'And he lost his children too!' Pippa said feelingly.

'*Sim*. A son and a daughter—and we lost, too, a beloved sister—and Carlos a wife.' Curiously, 'You know of this?' and, as Pippa nodded, Luisa went on— her homely, cheerful features momentarily downcast, 'The loss of a son is a great sorrow, Philippa, for now there is no one of our name to take over the wine house. For a proud man it is important to have a son—sons—to inherit his wealth, the family traditions, especially for families as old as the Monteiros and the de Alvarezes. Carlos ...'

But this interesting conversation could be pursued no longer, for the two men had returned, still discussing such topics as fermentation and saccharinometers.

'Carlos seems to know a lot about wine,' Pippa observed to Luisa, as they sat a little apart.

'*Sim!*' Luisa seemed surprised. 'Did you not know? He plays a great part in Portugal's wine-growing industry. He is on the board of many large companies and travels abroad in their interests. Felipe often envies him his health and strength, for besides all this, Carlos sits on many charitable committees. He is a man much loved and respected in our country.'

Pippa squirmed as she recalled her recent lecture to Carlos on the subject of leading a useful existence.

'You like Carlos, is it not so?' Luisa asked. Her eyes behind the dreadful spectacles were shrewd—too shrewd, Pippa thought, as too late she lowered her own from their introspection.

'Better than I thought I would,' she admitted.

'But enough to come to Portugal, to consider his offer? Inez said. . .'

Pippa flushed. How many more people knew about Carlos's present desire to mingle de Alvarez blood with de Alvarez blood, however diluted?

'I came to Portugal to work,' she told Luisa. 'If you're referring to marriage—he hasn't asked me . . .'

'But if he did, you would accept,' Luisa said positively, and before Pippa could protest, she went on, 'We shall look forward to you becoming a regular visitor in our house. Sometimes, we have feared Carlos would never marry again, and though we still mourn Carmela, we would not have him . . .'

'Philippa!' Carlos interrupted before matters could be set straight. 'Soon we must leave, if we are to complete our itinerary.'

He had scarcely finished speaking, to protests from the Monteiros, when sounds heralded the arrival of other visitors. The door of the *sala* opened to reveal Inez and Monty, come, they said, straight from Lisbon. Inez swept in with all the graceful assurance of the lovely woman, and seemed not to notice the cool though polite reception she received from Luisa. Why did Luisa dislike Inez so much?

Inez, Pippa had noticed at once, had eyes only for Felipe, and the jigsaw of the past began to fall into place. Thirteen years ago, Inez had left England in some urgency, so much so that she had not cared to spend time fighting for custody of her elder daughter. Thirteen years ago, Felipe had lost his wife and children. Inez was quite obviously a regular visitor at the Casa do Sol. It was all too pat to be mere coincidence. Felipe, she decided, was the man Inez de Alvarez loved, the reason that kept her only a convenient few miles away at Sintra.

But did Felipe return her affection? Studying him, Pippa found it hard to decide. There was no doubting his admiration of her as a beautiful woman, but she could detect nothing more in his manner.

Pippa's were not the only curious eyes. Monty, she discovered, was avidly surveying the trio of Luisa, Felipe and Inez, and Pippa thought she could read his mind. She had a sudden flash of insight. She knew the plot of Monty's projected novel. It would revolve around the triangle before her.

Monty, intuitive, but devious too, would have seen through every artifice to the heart of the matter and Inez, careless of who witnessed her volatile emotions, would have no suspicion that she was being used.

Much as Pippa still deprecated her mother's desertion of James Lang—and her loyalties still lay with her father, nothing she had learnt of Inez these past weeks had changed that—she still did not like to think of her mother's private life being used in the way Monty would use it. For he tore aside all veils, revealed naked emotions, leaving his victims no privacy of thought or action, and although his sources might be cunningly concealed he would, none the less, be making use of people to whom Pippa felt loyalty. For though she found she could not altogether like or approve of her mother—who in her way was as ruthless as the author himself—the ties of blood were still strong.

As for the Monteiros, Pippa had liked them at once. Felipe with his haggard handsomeness was a subject for compassion as well as admiration, while Luisa, plain in appearance, frank and forthright, appealed to Pippa's own straightforward nature.

Her discovery detracted a little from the pleasure of the visit, and she wasn't sorry when Carlos reminded her that they must depart, leaving Inez and Monty in possession of the field.

As Carlos drove, Pippa had much food for thought, her unpleasant conjecture as to the use Monty intended to make of Carlos's friends, but uppermost were thoughts of Carmela—Felipe and Luisa's sister—Carlos's wife. She wished there had been an opportunity to learn more about her. Luisa had described her as beautiful—had Carlos been madly in love with her, or had it been an 'arranged marriage' such as Carlos had spoken of that day at the Castelo dos Mouros?

She was so quiet that finally this drew comment from Carlos.

'You did not enjoy your visit to the Monteiros?'

'Oh yes, I did! Very much. I liked them immensely.'

'Then perhaps you did not find enough suitable background material for Senhor Mortimer's book? Perhaps I should have taken you around the winery?'

'Another time perhaps,' Pippa said absently. 'If

Monty asks for it.' Then, 'Carlos, Felipe Monteiro *is* the man, isn't he?'

He didn't pretend to misunderstand her.

'Twenty-four years ago, when Inez was Mariana's age, she fell in love with Felipe, *sim*. He was then already married. For a Portuguese girl of good upbringing she behaved with remarkable lack of discretion.'

Hence the remark 'like mother, like daughter', Pippa brooded, only she wasn't in love with a married man. Her heart gave the convulsive leap that always occurred whenever she allowed herself to dwell on her feeling for Carlos.

'Her father threatened her with an enforced stay in a convent, until the man he wished her to marry became of a suitable age.'

'A suitable age? He was younger than her? He . . .?' Pippa was nothing if not quick on the uptake. 'Her father wanted her to marry you?' she queried.

'*Sim*.' He smiled wryly. 'I was thirteen at the time, Inez eighteen. For her it would have meant a wait of at least five years. At eighteen, Inez was far more mature than Mariana. She had a ripeness, a promise of sensual beauty that I have only encountered once since . . .' His voice trailed away into thoughtfulness.

Pippa had not noticed the limousine drawing gradually to a halt. As Carlos applied the handbrake and turned to look speculatively at her, she became suddenly aware of his meaning, and instantly colour flooded her cheeks, while heat seemed to invade every part of her body.

'Carlos——' she began, her heart beating a nervous tattoo, but he shook his head in wry denial.

'Do not be afraid, Philippa. I have promised, have I not, no more distractions? At least,' his mouth widened into that bone-melting smile that he practised so rarely, 'at least, not at this moment.'

'Oh!' Relief? Disappointment? Pique? Which did she feel?

'Inez could not have the man she desired. She would not have the man her father wanted for her, so she ran away with a young Englishman, your father.' He shrugged. 'And for ten years, that was that.'

'Until thirteen years ago.'

'*Sim.* And then Maria Monteiro was killed in a road crash. Somehow Inez heard of it and she returned, quite without warning. Though I doubt she would have dared to do so had her father still been alive.'

'He never forgave her?'

'Never. As his only surviving male relative, I was his legal heir, but the monies he *could* have left to Inez, he chose to leave in trust for any children there might be of her marriage. He could not forget that they would be, in part, de Alvarez, as would be,' he looked at her searchingly, 'any children *you* might have?'

She evaded the issue.

'But it seems a bit pointless, my mother coming back here. Even though Felipe's free, she isn't.'

'As you say. But, as you so heatedly told me, for a woman there are many ways of loving. For Inez, it seems, it is sufficient that she see Felipe every day; and though I cannot approve, it says much for her devotion that she persists in her visits in the face of Luisa's disapproval, her constant presence. Inez and Felipe are never alone together for an instant.'

Philippa felt an unexpected pang of sympathy for her mother.

'Poor *Mãe.* But is Felipe in love with *her*?'

'I am not certain. Undoubtedly, he loved Maria. I doubt if in those days he even noticed the blatant adoration of an eighteen-year-old. But, in any case, he will never speak while your father lives. And, with Felipe's poor health, your father may well survive him.'

And, if Pippa surmised right, Monty knew all of this and would not hesitate to use it. She told Carlos of her fears, and was a little indignant when he smiled wryly at them.

'It isn't funny!' she snapped. 'These are real people— and they're friends of yours. Oh, Monty's used characters from life before, but . . .'

'But they weren't people personally known to you? Do not think, Philippa, that I defend Senhor Mortimer. I am only too aware of the unscrupulous way he has made use of de Alvarez hospitality. But there is nothing you or I can do about it.'

'You could ask him to leave your house,' she told him heatedly. 'Tell him you know what he's up to.'

'And he, *amada*, would deny it roundly. Have not you yourself said he is adept at disguising his sources? Besides,' he drawled softly, 'if he were to leave, would not you leave with him?'

Pippa parted her lips to say that was exactly what she was hoping for, then closed them again. That was before. Now she didn't want to leave Portugal. She didn't want to leave the Quinta de Estrella, but most of all, she didn't want to leave Carlos de Alvarez.

How dreadful, she thought. How history repeated itself! Her mother when young had been the victim of unrequited love, her devotion unnoticed, unwanted. She, Pippa, was older than Inez had been and Carlos wasn't married, but he was as unaware of her feelings as Felipe had been of Inez's. And just as well, she told herself firmly. How Carlos would laugh if he knew that, from absolute horror at the very thought of marrying him, she had passed into a state where it was a fate greatly to be desired.

Aware of his eyes on her, she returned to the safer subject of Monty's perfidy.

'Well, *I* shall tell him just what I think of him.'

Still Carlos seemed amused.

'That may afford you much personal satisfaction, but will it make any difference? I think not. But herein, my Philippa, lies the lesson I have tried to teach you. You, too, wish to become a writer, yet you deplore Senhor Mortimer's tactics. And I tell you, unless you are as willing to be unscrupulous in your use of people, you will never become as famous.'

'I don't agree.'

'I knew you would not. Nevertheless, I am right. But do not let us fight today, hmm? What do you say we finish our day by visiting the Quinta de Montserrate? A very strange property built at the whim of one of your own countrymen, its grounds laid out by Scottish landscape gardeners.'

Pippa agreed, simply and solely because she was reluctant for their day together to end.

The beauty of Montserrate, she discovered, lay not so much in the building with its Alhambra-like dome, but in its gardens, laid out, Carlos told her, at a time when travel was long and difficult; the seedlings that survived the journey planted outdoors in alien weather, to take root and grow into rare trees, shrubs and plants beside the simple plane tree and the hardy palm.

There were to be seen the greatest variety of ferns in the world, together with giant daturas, strawberry trees, bamboos, Chinese gingkos and monkey puzzles. Lovely vistas of waterfalls and lakes delighted the eye.

'At least everything we've seen today has been on

Monty's itinerary,' Pippa said with satisfaction, as they strolled around such incongruous architectural neighbours as a marble Turkish harem, Etruscan tombs, a fretwork chalet. Her pencil was constantly in use.

'Even though Senhor Monty is out of favour at the moment?'

'Yes.' She dimpled back at him, realising that, for the first time, she had smiled naturally at Carlos.

'And I, *amada*?' He was suddenly serious. 'Am I also out of favour? Do you still dislike me as much as ever?'

She blushed, her pulses quickening, but she couldn't lie.

'No. I think I like you a *little* better than when I first knew you,' she temporised. What an understatement!

The dark eyebrows rose quizzically heavenward.

'*Madre de Deus*, let us be thankful for small mercies. But? There is a "but"?'

'Yes,' she told him, bluntly frank. 'I can't *quite* like you when I remember the dreadful things you believed about me.'

'But I have apologised, have I not, for my mistakes?'

'I suppose so,' she said doubtfully. Had he?

'So has your opinion of me changed sufficiently for you to look more kindly on the idea of marrying me?'

Pippa gasped. She certainly hadn't expected their conversation to take this turn.

'But you . . .? You can't want to . . .?' she faltered.

'Can't I?' He was watching her face intently, his eyes, for once, not mocking her. 'Philippa . . .' For the self-assured Carlos de Alvarez, he spoke very hesitantly. 'Today's duty towards Senhor Mortimer now concluded, may I consider myself released from my promise?'

Not understanding, she looked at him questioningly.

'I think,' he explained softly, 'that now might not be an inappropriate moment for—*distractions*?'

For the last few hours, his promise making her feel safe, she had managed to banish the attraction he had for her to a distant corner of her mind. With his words, it was instantly at the forefront. The soft, caressing tone of his voice, his proximity reduced her to a not unfamiliar state of bemusement.

'Philippa, *tu queria*!' His soft, sensuous tone, as he took her hands in his, caused shivers to course the length of her spine, rendering her legs boneless, while at the same time she was filled with both a frantic desire to run away and the longing to be taken into his arms.

Hypnotised, she watched him as slowly, deliberately, he raised each of her hands in turn, kissed them. The warm masculine nearness of him as he used the gesture to draw her closer made her feel breathless and confused. The touch of his mouth on her hands seemed to leave behind a searing trail of heat which lasted long after his kisses had ceased.

'Am I released from my promise?' he persisted, and as she still could not answer him, he put his arms around her, the strength of his embrace both frightening and reassuring to her mixed emotions. She began to shake, but as his dark head came down towards her, she offered no resistance.

His lips only touched hers at first, softly outlining her mouth, particularly the full lower lip, tantalising kisses that made her long for a greater intensity of possession.

Then, just as she felt she must abandon pride and take the initiative, his mouth closed possessively over hers. She was drowning, lost in a welter of feeling. Desire raged through her and she clung fiercely to him, responding with all the strength of her own longing to the demands of his seeking tongue.

She was glad of the protection offered by the fret-work walls of the chalet, as his fingers first caressed then sought closer contact with the warm flesh of her swelling breasts. Her cry of arousal sounded loud in the roofed enclosure, and the thought that they might be over-heard, their embrace witnessed, restored her to some measure of sanity.

'No, Carlos—please!'

But he was obdurate, holding her firmly against him, denying her feeble struggles.

'Do not be afraid, my Philippa. This is behaviour that may be permitted of a *novio*, even in Portugal.'

'*Novio?*' she enquired breathlessly.

'Fiancé?'

'Oh, but . . .'

'Yes, Philippa,' he said decisively. 'We will be married.'

But, she thought confusedly, he didn't love her. So why?

CHAPTER SEVEN

WITH the madness of desire riding her, the tightly encircling arms making her weak, Pippa might well have said yes, but for that one consideration. Carlos didn't *love* her, but she knew why he was so determined to marry her. Mariana's vocation meant that she was his last, his only chance of marrying within the de Alvarez bloodline—and she *wouldn't* be used. Strange that he hadn't had this obsession, she mused, when he'd married Carmel Monteiro, and if his own story were to be believed, he had considered re-marriage, again outside the family. So why . . .?

'No, Carlos!' Firmly, she tried to disengage herself. 'We're not going to be married. I *won't* marry you.'

'But you would be making so many people happy *amada*,' he coaxed, his hands still caressing, his tone still complacent, as though he had anticipated a token denial, but was sure of a final surrender. 'Mariana, Inez and . . .' softly, the pressure of his body against hers increasing, 'and me.'

For happiness, she thought cynically, read 'achieving his obsessive ambition'. The vow of which Inez had told her—just how superstitious was Carlos? Was it possible that having once broken it, he had seen Carmela's death as retribution, that he hesitated to defy fate again?

'It wouldn't make my father happy,' she told him. 'He hates all the de Alvarez family. He'd be hurt and angry.'

'And for that you would refuse to marry me?' Carlos asked incredulously.

'Not just for that, no, though it must be a consideration. I love my father and he's been hurt enough by your
family. No, I've told you already, I don't ever want to
marry—not anyone.' But that had been before she'd
fallen in love with him. And she wished he would free
her from this tight clasp, the intimacy of which
threatened her resolve.

'You would rather go on working for Senhor
Mortimer?'

'No.' Pippa surprised even herself by the realisation of
this subconscious decision. 'I think the time has come
for me to prove myself as a writer—if I can.'

'You could combine a career as an author with
marriage,' he suggested.

'Oh, yes?' Pippa was sarcastic. 'In what little time I
had left from bearing and caring for *your sons*?'

For a moment she thought she saw a look of pain
distort his handsome face. But then she decided it must
be a trick of the sunlight filtering through the intricate
tracery of the fretwork chalet, for his tone was as even as
ever, as he replied, 'And you think so much of your
writing that you do not wish to be bothered with
children? Is that what happened to Senhor Makin's
child, Philippa? Your child—was he adopted?'

'No!' She shouted the word at him. She didn't want to
talk about that time, that subject any more. Suddenly,
Pippa felt utterly miserable. More so than if Carlos had
never proposed to her. At least that way she wouldn't
have experienced these awful feelings of self-doubt. Had
she done the right thing in refusing him? Loving him so
much, wanting him, wouldn't it have been better to
accept the half loaf he had to offer? In time, mightn't he
come to love the mother of the sons he craved? 'Can we
go now?' she asked, averting her face from him, so that

he couldn't see her unhappiness, trade on her inde-
cision, her longing.

'Very well!' he acceded stiffly, releasing her at last.
'But do not think, *amada*, that this subject is closed
between us. I will not accept your refusal.' Huskily, 'I
shall ask you again—and again.'

She could believe him capable of such persistence, but
was she as capable of repeated refusals—especially if he
accompanied his pressurising by the lovemaking at
which he was so adept? Might she not, in one of those
moments of weakness, say 'yes' instead of 'no'?

It was a relief to Pippa that there was a full complement
of diners around the de Alvarez table that evening, even
though she had little appetite and no inclination for
polite small talk.

Inez, however, had more than enough conversation,
and she and Monty kept up a running duologue on their
trip to Lisbon, as well as the visit to the Monteiros.

'And how did you like Felipe?' Inez asked her
daughter, when, as usual, the ladies had retired to the
sala and Mariana had gone over to the piano.

'I thought him a very nice man,' Pippa said
truthfully, and not just from a wish to please Inez. 'Such
a shame about his accident, losing his sister, Carlos's
wife. Why didn't you tell me, *Mãe*, that Carlos had been
married before? And Felipe lost his own wife and
children too,' she went on with additional emphasis,
watching her mother closely.

'*Sim.*' Inez met Pippa's eyes with a trace of defiance. 'I
suppose you have guessed how it is with me? Luisa, of
course, has always known and she hates me—dreadful
woman.'

'Luisa? Dreadful?' Pippa exclaimed. '*I* don't think

she's dreadful. I liked her. She's so devoted to her brother and ...'

'Devoted!' Inez face darkened. 'She is possessive. She hates me because she is afraid—afraid that some day, somehow, it will be possible for Felipe and I to be together, and she knows that then she must leave.'

'You wouldn't throw Luisa out?' Pippa was shocked. 'Anyway, I'm sure Felipe wouldn't, not after all she's done for him. Besides, the only way you could be together—in the way you mean—is if something happened to Dad.'

'Sim.' Inez said carelessly and Pippa was again horrified by her callousness.

'Wouldn't you care at all?' she demanded. 'After all, you were married, lived with him for ten years, had his children. Surely that must count for something?'

'When I am with Felipe,' Inez said passionately, dark eyes smouldering, 'nothing else in the world matters.'

'Including me—and Mariana,' Pippa recognised bitterly. 'Since you're so willing to sacrifice either one of us to Carlos's mad schemes.'

'Oh, that!' Inez shrugged airily. 'Since he could not marry me, Carlos made a vow to your grandfather that some day, if I had daughters, he would marry one of you, when you were old enough. He broke that vow once in marrying Carmela Monteiro but he will not break it again, I think. And since Mariana is so foolish as to throw away her chance, then it must be you.' She spoke as if it were merely a matter of logic, Pippa thought indignantly, and not of people's lives—how callous she had sounded in speaking of the dead Carmela. But Pippa was aghast, too, at her mother's hypocrisy. Though Inez had confirmed Pippa's own conjecture, she spoke as if Carlos had been justly punished for breaking his vow, but what of the vows Inez herself had taken? Marriage vows. And there was more:

'*You* refused to be married off to the man your father chose for you,' she pointed out. 'Why should I be any different? For one thing, I've been brought up in England, to be independent, and for another, I'm *your* daughter. You rebelled, why shouldn't I refuse to go along with your schemes? I would have expected you to be pleased about Mariana. It's your religion too, and Carlos says ...'

'A religion that all these years has kept me apart from the man I wanted,' Inez snapped. 'For ten years I attended Mass every day, prayed to God that somehow Felipe and I might be together one day, and how has he answered me? Oh yes, he freed Felipe, but in what a fashion? A man paralysed from the waist down. And I— I am still not free to be with him totally.'

The impassioned outburst came as a shock to her daughter. She didn't share her mother's religion, but somehow it didn't seem right to her that Inez should speak so angrily, so critically of the God she claimed to believe in. Was this why Inez was now less assiduous in the practice of her religion? Because, despite her arrogance, even she could not deny that she was erring against its precepts?

Pippa was glad when Carlos and Monty joined them and the conversation became general, and it was only later that she realised Inez had not answered her question. Why hadn't her mother told her of Carlos's earlier marriage?

Because she feared the effect of Carlos's threatened persistence, Pippa refused steadfastly to accompany him on any more excursions, even resisting the lure of the promised trip to Alcobaça. But she was not, after all, to be disappointed of that particular treat.

She had made several visits to the Monteiros since her
first, not with Carlos, but with Inez. She hadn't
deliberately sought her mother's company. She was
totally disillusioned by what she'd learnt recently of
Inez's character. But Luisa had telephoned several times
with flatteringly pressing invitations and since Pippa
would not accept Carlos's escort, she must perforce—
unless she wanted to offend Luisa—accompany Inez on
her visits to the Casa do Sol.

Though she liked the Monteiros more with each
succeeding encounter, the visits were not exactly
comfortable occasions. On the drive there, Inez would
be in a state of febrile excitement, on their return home
in the depths of depression, complaining bitterly of
Luisa's ever-watchful presence.

'I cannot say a word to Felipe that she doesn't hear. I
would have thought, Philippa,' she reproached 'that you
could have taken her from the room for a while on some
pretext.'

'Why should I?'

It was strange, Pippa thought wryly, that she who had
rebelled so strenuously against Carlos's strictures on
seemly behaviour, now sympathised with Luisa's rigid
propriety.

During one of these visits to the Casa do Sol, Luisa
quietly suggested to Pippa that she might care to go
away with her and Felipe for a few days.

'We go away from home rarely. Travelling is not easy
for him, even though one of the limousines has been
adapted for his chair. But four times a year, we to go
Caldas da Rainha, so that Felipe may take the waters. It
is not far from Alcobaça. So while . . .'

'Alcobaça!' Pippa exclaimed. 'But how marvellous!

Carlos said ...' She stopped. She didn't visit the Monteiros with Carlos and she had all too sedulously avoided mention of his name. 'I'd love to go with you,' she finished awkwardly.

'*Bom*! Say nothing to your mother,' Luisa warned, 'or she will undoubtedly insist on accompanying you—though not,' she added drily, 'for your sake.'

Just as Pippa was wondering how, without Inez's co-operation, she was supposed to travel from Sintra to Colares—for neither would she seek Carlos's help—Luisa added, 'We will send the second car for you.'

On the morning of her departure, Pippa was on tenterhooks. She had packed a small suitcase and this was concealed in her room. She had told no one she was leaving the Quinta for a few days and in her guilty awareness it seemed to her that the others would never go about their own affairs, Inez and Monty to Lisbon once more, Carlos to wherever his business or charity work usually took him.

With a sigh of relief, she saw Monty and Inez off, but irritatingly, Carlos showed no signs of leaving and soon the Monteiros's limousine would be calling for her.

Just as she was steeling herself to leave under Carlos's nose, with all the consequent explanations and, quite possibly, recriminations, the telephone rang and he went to answer it.

Fingers crossed, Pippa hoped that the call would either keep him engaged or call him away urgently. But Carlos was only occupied for two or three minutes and still there was no sign of her transport.

'That was Luisa,' Carlos said and Pippa looked at him apprehensively. 'Unfortunately, she is unable to send the other limousine. It has developed a mechanical fault.

Come—fetch your suitcase.'

Without giving her an opportunity to answer, he strode from the room and a somewhat dazed Pippa went to do as he bade.

Luisa must have told him of their plans and somehow talked him into driving Pippa to Colares. She must have been very persuasive and tactful, Pippa marvelled, for Carlos hadn't seemed at all put out that she was leaving.

The first part of the drive was accomplished in total silence until Pippa decided that it would be churlish of her not to make some acknowledgement of his help, which might, after all, be causing him some inconvenience, making him late for an appointment.

'This is very kind of you,' she said hesitantly, with a nervous sideways glance at his austere profile, then found herself quite unable to drag her gaze away from the features she had come to love.

'Not at all.' There was veiled amusement in the glance he shot her and Pippa supposed he found humour in the fact that she was obliged to be polite to him.

Luisa came bustling to meet them and Carlos offered to assist with the stowing away of luggage, to help get Felipe and his chair into the back of the converted limousine.

With everything in readiness, last moment instructions issued to servants for her absence, Luisa finally announced that they could leave.

The conversion of the limousine had left only the long bench seat at the front for other passengers, Luisa, Pippa and the driver. Luisa urged Pippa to enter first.

'You are more agile than I. Besides you are slim. You will not mind sitting between us?'

Pippa had no objection whatsoever until, to her consternation, she realised that Carlos was taking the driver's place behind the wheel.

'What are you doing?' she demanded.

'Isn't that self-evident?' he asked mockingly.

'Carlos always drives us to Alcobaça,' Luisa put in with an air of innocence that Pippa knew at once was assumed. 'Did you not know?'

'No!' Pippa snapped. 'I didn't and if I had ...' She stopped, aware that she was on the brink of discourtesy to the Monteiros.

'And if you had?' Carlos enquired, that irritating note of amusement still in his voice.

'Nothing!' she muttered.

The road from Colares to the north continued through vineyards that stretched over the rolling hills as far as the eye could see. Rising majestically above the beautiful Caeiras vineyards, was the medieval walled town of Obidos, its square castle and great weather-beaten towers making it seem like an enormous grounded vessel.

'Another of Alfonso Henriques's conquests,' Carlos observed to an unresponsive Pippa. She had determined not to speak to him.

Crushed as she was between him and Luisa, she might refuse to speak, but to ignore his presence was another matter. However she tried to edge further towards Luisa, sooner or later a bend in the road would force her thigh, her shoulder, once more against his, so that she was continually, agonisingly aware of him—first his aura of warm masculinity, then her own withdrawal from it, nearly as painful in its sense of loss.

Their route did not pass through Obidos, but ran on towards Caldas da Rainha. The name, Carlos explained, seemingly oblivious of Pippa's deliberate silence, meant 'the Queen's Thermal Baths'.

'Since the last century, Caldas has been the most popular hot springs resort in Portugal. It is fortunate for Felipe that it is no distance from us at Sintra.'

With Felipe deposited at the hospital associated with the famous spa, Carlos drove on farther north. Luisa had reserved rooms for them for two or three days at a *pensão* actually in Alcobaça, in the same square as the famous monastery Pippa longed to see.

By the time they had unpacked and settled into their rooms, it was a little too late for sightseeing. With the advance of winter, the daylight was growing shorter, and Pippa heard with relief that Carlos had promised to drive back to Caldas to see that Felipe was comfortable, while Luisa seemed happy to settle down for a cosy chat.

'It is so nice to be able to speak without Inez present. I hope I do not offend you, my dear Philippa, but these days I cannot like your mother.' She sighed. 'Though as girls we were very close indeed.'

Instantly, Pippa disclaimed any offence.

'She's my mother and I wouldn't wish her any harm, but I'm afraid she *isn't* a very likeable person. I've come to the conclusion my father is better off without her.'

'I doubt he sees it like that,' Luisa remarked. 'Men can be so blinded by a beautiful woman.' Was Felipe blinded by Inez's beauty to her real character?

'Oh, I don't know,' Pippa said thoughtfully. 'I think he's got over it after all this time. He's had women friends since she left. In fact, he's quite friendly now with one of the teachers at the school I used to go to. I sometimes wish he'd divorce *Mãe* and get married again. After all, he's still young. I suppose that shocks you, Luisa? The idea of him divorcing *Mãe*?'

'Shocks? *Não*! I know, of course, that this is done in your country. If it is not against his conscience, I agree your father is entitled to some happiness. But in our eyes it would still not free Inez to marry Felipe, for that is what *she* desires. But let us not talk of your mother. For once we are free of her. Let us talk of you—and Carlos.'

Pippa frowned: She was both eager and reluctant to discuss Carlos. This woman had known him so much longer, must know more about him than she, things Pippa longed to know. She felt, too, that she owed Luisa some explanation of her churlish behaviour on the journey.

'You must have noticed, Luisa,' she said hesitantly, 'that I wasn't very pleased when I found Carlos was coming with us.'

'*Sim*. But then I also knew there had been some coolness between you and Carlos of late. You will not think me impertinent if I ask? You have quarrelled?'

'Not quarrelled exactly. But there is something we disagree on. Luisa,' she said earnestly, 'I have to discuss this with someone. Mariana is too unworldly. It would worry her. Besides, she wouldn't understand how I feel. And I can't—I won't talk to my mother about. . .'

'I should be honoured,' Luisa said simply.

'Carlos asked me to marry him that day, on the way back from your home.'

'I thought he would. But you refused him, I think?'

'Yes.' Then, desperately, 'Luisa, he wants to marry me for the wrong reasons. He doesn't love me . . .'

'As you love him . . .?'

'Yes—well—that's . . . But *he* wants to marry *me* only because I'm half de Alvarez, because of a silly promise he made to my grandfather—so that our children. . .'

'Children?' Luisa interrupted. '*Desculpe-me*,

Philippa. But that is not possible.

'Not—not possible?' Pippa queried. 'We are only very distantly related, you know?'

'*Não! Não!* I mean it is not possible for Carlos to have children. That is another bond between him and Felipe—a great sorrow. No one to inherit his fortune, his family traditions.'

Pippa stared at her uncomprehendingly.

'But my mother said that was why ...'

'Philippa,' Luisa said gravely, 'I would question very earnestly anything Inez may have told you.' She hesitated, then continued, '*Madre de Deus*, what am I thinking of, to consider discussing such things with a young unmarried girl, I who have also never married. But since you have chosen me as your confidante ...'

'It's all right, honestly,' Pippa reassured her. 'I don't mind. I'm not embarrassed. That's if *you* don't mind ...?'

'But of course—the English!' Luisa spread her capable hands in acknowledgement of their eccentric ways. 'Then I will tell you. Carlos and Carmela had no children of their marriage of many years. The doctors, they say it is Carlos, a childhood illness, *esta percebido?* They say it will leave him ... *como se diz?*'

'Sterile?' Pippa hazarded.

'*Sim! Sim!*' Luisa nodded vigorously.

Poor, poor Carlos, Pippa brooded, a thrill of compassion pervading her whole being, so that she felt weak with love for him. What a blow that must have been to his sense of dynasty, but also to his masculine pride. But now inevitably other considerations came to the fore—suppose, still in ignorance of his inability to father children, she had agreed to marry him? How was he to know *she* did not fervently desire to be a mother some day? By keeping her in ignorance, he would have robbed her of the right to decide for herself if she were willing to sacrifice motherhood.

'Would it matter to you?' Luisa probed gently, 'that there will be no children if you marry Carlos?'

'No,' Pippa remarked slowly. Despite her momentary anger at the deception it seemed he would have practised on her, her love for Carlos *was* great enough to encompass such a disappointment. But that wasn't the point—*would* he have gone on deceiving her if Luisa hadn't spoken out?

But her own indignation apart, why on earth, Pippa puzzled, was Carlos making such a thing of marrying someone of de Alvarez blood, since the line could never be perpetuated? She voiced her thoughts.

'It has never occurred to you, Philippa,' Luisa asked gently, 'that Carlos loves you?'

It hadn't until now, when his only other motive for wanting to marry her seemed to have been swept aside. Perhaps *that* was why he hadn't confided in her? Fearing to lose her? *That* she could forgive.

'Do you really think . . .?'

'*Sim.* I have seen it in his face, heard it in his voice, when he speaks to you, of you.'

In that case, Pippa mused, Luisa must be far more observant than she, for she had detected no such emotion. Desire, yes, but love? She shook her head doubtfully. Until he spoke of love—until he was honest with her . . . But conjecture kept her wide awake, far into the night.

Pippa found it a little embarrassing to meet Carlos next morning with her new knowledge of such an intimate factor in his life, its consequent effect upon her view of his motives. She had confidently expected that Luisa would make a third on their sightseeing, but the older woman stated quite categorically that she had shopping to do, acquaintances to visit.

Was it because Pippa was English that Luisa felt chaperonage was unnecessary, or had she succumbed to Carlos's persuasion? Pippa had her suspicions.

It was market day in Alcobaça and at every turn there was something fresh to catch the eye—stalls of bright dress lengths, hardware, glass, china, foodstuffs. A tie vendor bore on his shoulders a long pole from which dangled ties of every colour.

But there was no doubt about their prime target and Pippa found herself meekly accompanying Carlos across the square, towards the light beige façade she had only caught a glimpse of yesterday.

The interior of the abbey was austerely empty, the ascetic rules of the Cistercians, Carlos explained, but in the Sala dos Tumulos were the tombstones they had come to see. Here, supported by six lions, lay the crowned Dom Pedro, serious of face, with a curly beard and long hair, his hands clasping a sword, spurs on his feet. Beside Pedro's tomb, bathed in the filtered silvery light from an arched window, the uncrowned queen reposed on a stony pillow, watched over by six angels with outspread wings.

'It was Pedro's wish to be buried here, alongside his beloved Inez. Two children were born of their love. But malicious courtiers murdered her. When he came to the throne, Pedro had his revenge. He had the murderers delivered to him, their hearts torn out.'

It was an awesome, tragic, but also a bloodthirsty tale. Pippa shuddered as Carlos went on to tell how Pedro had had Inez's corpse brought from her tomb, dressed in

silks and cloth of gold, placed on the throne beside him
and forced his courtiers to kiss her fleshless hands.

'Now you know something of the lengths to which
passion *can* drive a man,' Carlos said as, the rest of the
building an anticlimax, they strolled out into the
daylight once more.

'It's rather frightening,' Pippa told him. 'I don't
think I'd want to be loved with that kind of intensity. I
like men to be gentle.'

'And do you not think Pedro *was* gentle in his loving
of Inez?' Carlos enquired softly. 'As *I* would be in my
loving of *you*?' His guiding hand had steered her
towards the Monteiros limousine and, before she had
realised it, he had seated her and was driving away, out
of the city.

'Wh-where are we going?' she stammered. His
words had unnerved her.

'To a place,' he told her, increasing her apprehension,
'where we can be alone for once.'

Nazaré, some ten miles from Alcobaça, was an alluring
village given over entirely to fishing. But now in
November the strange local boats, long, narrow,
brightly coloured, the 'Eye of God' painted on every
stem-post, were pulled right up off the beach into the
streets and squares of the little town to protect them
from the Atlantic gales. There they would remain until
spring returned.

Narrow straight streets ran down steeply from the
inland heights to the sea front, and here Carlos parked
the limousine, suggesting they walk for a while.

A stiffish breeze was blowing off the sea, fresh and
invigorating rather than unpleasant. But wind and tide
could both be treacherous, Carlos told Pippa.

'This coast has widowed many a fisherman's wife.'

'Why didn't you tell me you knew about this trip?' Pippa asked as they climbed to Sitio, the other half of Nazaré, a cluster of white stone cottages poised precariously on formidable cliffs. 'Why didn't you tell me you were coming too?'

'Would you have come if I had?'

'Probably not. No.' She admitted.

'There you have your answer. I wanted this time with you, Philippa.' He stopped, looking down at her. 'Soon the Senhor plans to return to England. I do not wish you to leave with him.'

'But you know I will—I *must.*'

'There is no *must* about it. You do not wish to work for the Senhor any longer. So there is no reason why you should not stay here with me, as my wife.'

'Carlos, I—oh please, don't.' Pippa's voice trailed away and she stared blindly at the view, anywhere but at him. The knowledge she had gained from Luisa had weakened her resolve to resist him; her heart yearned over the disappointment he must feel at being unable to have the children he so much desired, the sadness he must have known at the loss of his wife. But she couldn't forget that he *had* once been married, that he had still not told her there would be no children of a marriage between them. In love there must be total honesty, trust ... And what about her career?

From the precipitous clifftop, miles of shelving, glittering white sands curved away to a distant promontory. The sea, flowing in vast rolling waves the length of the bay, smoothed out and eradicated every mark as they slid up the sand with deceptive speed and power. Pippa felt as if she were also on the edge of an emotional precipice, contemplating an invisible, unpredictable horizon. Mightn't an involvement with Carlos prove as dangerous as those mighty waves below her? She could be in danger of letting the power of his attraction for her sweep away, as if they had never been, her plans and ambitions for the future.

'Pippa!'

Startled, she turned to look at him. It was the first time he has ever used the abbreviation of her name and the way he said it, it sounded like an endearment.

'Pippa, *mi amada*, so much perhaps has been said to you of our family history, the blood we share, that perhaps not enough has been said of feelings?'

CHAPTER EIGHT

YOU see, *mi amada*,' he went on, 'I know how it is with you.'

Pippa stiffened, as though she had received a slap in the face. No mention on his part of any feeling for her. And what gave him the colossal self-assurance to assume that she . . .? What had he ever done, what effort had he made to make her even like him, let alone fall in love with him? That she had done so was merely the foolishness of her own rebellious heart and body. And so she retorted, 'You know nothing of the sort.'

'You deny that you want me?' His voice was soft, caressing, but still there was that undertone of incredulous amusement, a spark of it in his eyes that set her alight with fiery pride.

'I do deny it!' With no words of love exchanged between them she would not admit to *desire*.

The mockery vanished suddenly and the expression that replaced it provoked in Pippa an instinctive trembling, as she anticipated his next move, but too late to prevent it.

With one arm around her, his free hand beneath her chin, tilting her face up towards him, his penetrating scrutiny seemed unending. She trembled under that gaze as it seemed to plumb the very depths of her and she knew the quivering that racked her was only giving the lie to her denial.

'Your lips tell me so—but your body tells a different story.'

His mouth took hers in a kiss of ruthless possession.

She fought fiercely at first. Then, when it was obvious he would not release her until he was ready to do so, she allowed herself to slacken in his grasp, her mouth still and cold.

But it was a mistake. He took advantage of her limpness to mould every inch of her to the hardness of him. His tongue invaded the soft, trembling lips, finally evoking a response all her determination could not quell until, moaning helplessly, she returned his kisses, clung desperately to the support of his muscular frame.

When she felt as though she must faint under the intensity of her sensations, he lifted his dark head, looking once more into her now bemused, dilated grey eyes.

'Now tell me you do not care for me.' His quiet laugh was, nevertheless, a triumphant sound and that note of complacence broke the spell under which he had placed her.

At that moment it was impossible for Pippa to tell where one emotion ended and the other began.

'I think,' she told him tremulously, 'that I *hate* you.

'May I ask who gave you leave to take time off?' This from Monty.

'And pray, why wasn't I invited to accompany you?' This, Inez.

Immediately upon her return to the Quinta de Estrella, Pippa became the object of a two-pronged attack.

She had been both glad and sorry when the visit to Alcobaça was over. Since her rejection of Carlos on the hilltop at Sitio, he had been quiet and withdrawn, the further onslaughts she had feared upon her defences not forthcoming, and she was glad to be out of his disturbing presence. But there was sorrow too, for her sojourn in

Portugal was nearly over.

Whether or not Monty intended to stay on, she knew that *she* could not. Quite simply she couldn't afford to stay. If she was going to leave Monty's employ to give herself more freedom for her own writing, she would need at least part-time employment until she discovered if it were possible to live by her pen.

Inez and Monty, each usually so formally polite in the other's presence, were seething with the accumulated annoyance of several days. Unable as hostess and guest to vent their spleen upon each other, they chose Pippa as their target.

'I return home to find only a brief note telling me of your whereabouts,' Inez complained. 'The Monteiros are ...' She corrected herself. 'Felipe is *my* friend. You had no business accepting an invitation that did not include me.'

And Pippa, herself still emotionally raw, retorted with some force.

'You wouldn't have been invited anyway. Luisa wanted me *without you*.'

Inez gasped her affront. The plump figure bridled. Probably no one had ever taken such a tone to her.

'How dare you speak to me, your mother, so?'

'Oh, *Mãe*, come off it,' Pippa said wearily. 'You must know you forfeited all rights in that respect when you walked out of my life. Where I go, what I do, who I see is none of your concern.'

But Inez had rallied and her expression became one of almost malicious triumph.

'Maybe not. Your father may not have seen fit to curb you, but a husband certainly will. Your behaviour will be Carlos's concern when you are married to him.'

'Pippa to marry Carlos?' The words emerged shrilly from Monty's slackened jaw and his monocle toppled from its ocular perch. 'Is this true, Pippa?' he demanded.

'No, it's not,' she said irritably, 'and even if it were, it's no one's business except mine. Since you're so concerned about the time I've had off, I'll go and get on with some work. But it's only fair to warn you, Monty, that when I've made up for the lost time, I'll be giving you a week's notice.' She stalked out before he could make any rejoinder or protest.

And for the next two or three days Pippa did work, feverishly, stopping only to eat and sleep. She saw Carlos rarely and when she did he was distant and formal, so that she tried to tell herself she'd been right to turn down his proposal. His present behaviour showed just how little he cared for her personally.

Monty's manuscript was taking the direction she'd anticipated and something within her shrank from his dissection of three people she now knew so well. She was glad *her* interest lay in history. She could never use anyone so.

The only incident which broke up the monotony of the work that had become distasteful to her was the quiet ceremony involved in Mariana's acceptance as a novice into the Convent of Santa Eulalia. Only family and close friends were invited, limiting the congregation to those from the Quinta de Estrella and the Casa do Sol.

Felipe Monteiro did not look well, Pippa registered. He hadn't received as much benefit as usual from his visit to Caldas da Rainha, Luisa told her in a quiet aside, and Pippa noticed that Luisa's attention was more concerned with her brother than with the short service of initiation.

Understandably the Monteiros refused an invitation to return afterwards to the Quinta for the small family celebration.

'It's *her* doing, of course,' Inez said bitterly. 'Luisa would refuse anything that gave me a few more hours of Felipe's company.'

'Are you blind?' Pippa demanded incredulously. 'Couldn't you see he wasn't feeling well, that she wanted to get him home as soon as possible?'

'Felipe not well!' Inez tried to scoff. 'Ridiculous! He has the constitution of an ox.' But her tone was uneasy and the anxious widening of her eyes, the sudden quivering of her lips belied her would-be confident tone, and she was very quiet all evening.

Though a sense of the gentle, introspective Mariana's presence had been all but negligible, Pippa missed her sister. Without Mariana, some of the inhibitions imposed by her unworldliness disappeared and tempers seemed ragged all round.

Inez fretted and fumed because, constantly, her calls at the Casa do Sol were frustrated. Servants informed her that their master was not able to receive visitors.

'*She* is keeping him from me!' was her constant cry.

Monty flatly refused to accept that Pippa was determined to quit his employ. The very idea had thrown him into a state approaching panic and Pippa began to realise, somewhat belatedly, just how much of his recent success had been due to her contribution to his work. He was irritable and petulant by turns.

And Carlos. He was rarely at home. Pippa suspected that he alone was permitted to visit Felipe Monteiro's sick bed, but much as she longed to ask after the invalid, she could not bring herself to approach Carlos in order to ask.

Nor was Pippa happy. Since her arrival at the Quinta, she had kept her promise to her father that she would keep in touch. As she had expected, he was hurt and angry to learn her whereabouts and to placate him it had taken countless assurances that she'd been totally ignorant of her destination, of Monty and Inez's compact. Even so, in every letter, James Lang demanded to know when Pippa would be returning home. If this minor involvement of hers with the de Alvarez family had so upset him, she could not imagine the depths of his anguish were she to write and tell him she planned to *marry* Carlos. But that wouldn't be necessary.

It was her misfortune that there would be no tidy happy ending to her first genuine encounter with love. Her first and her last, she suspected miserably. For where in the world was there a man who could match up to Carlos, to his attraction for her?

Pippa was not a light sleeper and it took a lot to rouse her in the small hours of the morning. But the cry that echoed around the walls of the Quinta de Estrella shortly after midnight a week after Mariana had entered the noviciate would, she thought, have aroused all but the sleeping dead.

The very thought made her shiver, for the cry had all the anguish of a soul in torment, and she slid hurriedly from her warm bed, pulling a wrap about her as she trembled with the dread of something unknown.

By the time she reached the ground floor, the Quinta was astir. Monty, long grey hair tousled—Pippa had never before seen him anything but immaculately coiffeured—stood in the tiled hallway, clutching a flamboyant oriental dressing-gown around his tall spare frame.

Inez, wild of eye and dress, was there supported by Carlos. He was as flawlessly attired as usual, but drawn of face. It was Inez who had cried out and she continued to sob hysterically, as a servant appeared to say that the Senhora's limousine was ready.

'Come with me, Carlos?' It was the first time Pippa had heard her imperious mother beg for anything. 'I cannot bear it alone.'

'Of course,' was his quiet reply.

'What's happening, Monty?' Pippa turned to her only remaining source of information.

'Monteiro! Dying!' he said brusquely. 'Shocking thing—only fifty-seven.' The septuagenarian's own gaunt face was pale with this sudden realisation of mortality.

'Oh, how awful!' Pippa's eyes filled with tears. But her pain was not at that moment for Inez's anguish, but for Felipe himself, that quiet, gentle man who had already suffered so much loss and now was to lose his own life—and what about Luisa? Felipe was her whole world. All Inez's concern would be for Felipe, for herself, but who would care for Luisa's feelings?

Carlos would, she realised with a pang of relief. He would, she thought, with a sense of surprise that she had not recognised it before, be a rock to cling to in any crisis. That the Monteiros had relied on him heavily for many things had already become apparent to Pippa during her brief acquaintance with them.

'Well, I'm going back to bed,' Monty pronounced. It was obvious that he had suddenly realised how far his appearance was departed from its *soigné* norm. 'I can't afford to have my rest interrupted like this.'

Typical Monty, Pippa thought, selfish to the last. It was amazing to realise how much she had learnt about him in a few short weeks. The background of the Quinta, his interreaction with the people there, had revealed many unpleasant facets of his nature, traits which had not been evident in three years of working with him in his own environment.

'You'd better do the same!' Monty's impatient words

broke in on Pippa's train of thought and she looked at him blankly.

'Do what?'

'Get back to bed, of course,' he said testily. 'Tomorrow will be a working day the same as usual. Monteiro's death has nothing to do with you and I.'

Fortunately he didn't wait to see if she complied with his injunction, for the look Pippa gave him would have out-Gorgoned the Medusa! With Monty's disappearance towards his own quarters, Pippa wandered wearily into the *sala*. There was no way she could go back to bed, to sleep, and forget the tragedy now being enacted at the Casa do Sol.

Suddenly she found herself weeping for the gentle Felipe, weeping for Luisa, about to lose the only man that self-avowed spinster heart had ever loved. She fell asleep with the traces of tears still upon her face.

And here Carlos found her, the lights of the *sala* still burning above her unconscious head, when he returned, several hours later—alone.

'Pippa!'

Just her name, but at the mere sound of his voice, she, the heavy sleeper, woke instantly and jumped to her feet.

'Oh! Carlos! What time is it? Goodness, I must have fallen asleep.' Then, remembering—'Felipe?' she faltered.

A shadow of pain crossed his features, the greyness of their fatigue relieved only by the unkempt blue-black of his unshaven jaw-line.

'It is all over,' he said simply.

'Oh, Carlos, I'm so sorry.' Instinctively, she went straight into his arms, not just to be comforted but to comfort.

For a moment he held her closely to him, straining her against his lean muscularity as if he would never release her, and she felt a response stir in him before, almost brusquely, he set her aside.

'Not now,' he muttered. 'Forgive me, but I must bathe and change. There are many arrangements to be made.'

'Carlos!' At his name, spoken pleadingly, he looked back at her, the brilliant glaze of her grey eyes making him halt irresolute upon the threshold.

'You have been crying,' he said wonderingly. 'I did not expect that you would care so much.'

'Of course I care.' Pippa was indignant. 'H-how is Luisa?'

'Devastated.' The spread of his hands amply demonstrated Luisa's sense of loss.

'I wish I could go to her.'

'Do you?' He did come back into the room then, looking down at her with a strange intensity. 'Why?'

'Because I like her—I'm very fond of her. I feel she's already a friend. And now she has no one—except you, of course.'

'She has Inez,' he said surprisingly.

'*Mãe*?' Pippa was frankly incredulous. 'But ...?'

Sighing wearily, he sat down, drawing her with him. He studied her face as he spoke, searching for—what?

'You could not know, of course. As children, Luisa and Inez were very close. They were at the same convent school. They shared everything, dreams, friends, clothes, until, when Inez was eighteen and Luisa twenty, Inez fell in love with Luisa's married brother. Her ridiculous, indiscreet behaviour at that time alienated the whole Monteiro family, including Luisa, who loved her sister-in-law, worshipped her small nephew and niece as if they were her own. She feared the effect of Inez's wild, irresponsible behaviour upon her brother's marriage. She need not have worried, since

Felipe never falterd in his adoration of his Maria. But even then Inez was a woman obsessed. She and Luisa quarrelled bitterly.'

'And that obsession lasted throughout ten years of marriage and beyond,' Pippa marvelled. 'Is such a thing really possible?'

'I told you,' Carlos said, with an odd note to his voice, 'that you knew nothing of the heights, the depths of passion.'

'And when *Mãe* came back to Portugal? After Maria's death? What then?'

'Luisa could not physically prevent her calling at the Casa. Besides, Felipe was glad of any diversion from his unhappiness, his pain. And he was too kind to snub the woman who patently adored him. But now Luisa was terrified that because he was so alone, he would fall in love with Inez and be hurt again—because Inez was not free. And her beloved brother had suffered pain enough.'

'Poor Luisa—poor Felipe.' Pippa's eyes sparkled with unshed tears and Carlos spoke almost absently as he watched her expressive face. 'What now?' she asked.

'Now Inez remains with Luisa—at Felipe's own wish.' As Pippa looked at him enquiringly, 'Felipe was not blind—he was not unaware of Inez's feelings, of how matters stood between her and his sister. I genuinely believe, however, that he was never in love with Inez, that his heart lay buried with his Maria and his children. It is possible for a man to love so ...'

Carlos stopped. His voice had thickened curiously and Pippa looked at him in wonder, witnessing his momentary loss of control. Was he thinking of his dead wife—Carmela? Tentatively she laid a hand on his arm, to have it grasped fiercely in both of his.

'Felipe,' he went on in that oddly altered voice, 'was

kindness to the last. He knew he was dying. Inez was at his bedside at his personal request. It must have cost him a great effort, but he took the hand of each woman and ...' Again Carlos's voice quivered. Pippa had not believed this arrogant man capable of such deep emotions and she waited patiently, her eyes on his dark head, downbent over the hand he held so tightly, her heart yearning over him. 'He said, "After my death I want only friendship and understanding between— between those I love!"'

Carlos fell silent, his story finished, but Pippa whispered;

'So he let *Mãe* think that he *did* love her after all! Oh, Carlos! What—what a good kind man he was. I wish—I wish ...' She broke down, the long-threatened tears spilling over, and it seemed only right and natural that she and Carlos, with a grief shared, should hold together in close understanding of each other's needs.

'My God! Then it's true!'

It was Pippa who jerked upright and away at the sound of Monty's exclamation. Carlos viewed the still *deshabillé* figure of the author with regained composure.

'True, *senhor*?' he enquired. 'What is true?' He rose, but unhurriedly.

'About you and Pippa. Dona Inez said—I could hardly believe such nonsense. You, my girl,' he said severely to Pippa, 'should know better. How many times have I told you, a writer needs total dedication to his art. You can't afford distractions.'

'You've told me so hundreds of times,' Pippa agreed, 'but,' sarcastically, 'the "dedication" you demanded was to your work, not mine. Like a fool, I've only just realised that.'

'And this ...' Monty ignored her accusation, 'is how you intend to repay me for all I've taught you? I should have known a woman would be dazzled by all this,' he gestured disdainfully around him, 'the trappings of wealth, the pseudo-aristocracy bit—friend of kings, indeed! Bah!'

'All you've taught me,' Pippa retorted, on her feet now, and so incensed that she was quite oblivious of an interestedly listening Carlos, 'is how to batten on other people's lives, suck their stories, their innermost feelings out of them, like some—some disgusting old vampire. You've never had a genuine emotion in your life—it's all second-hand. I realise now,' she swept on, 'how you've made use of me all these years. You've kept me on for your own purposes, not to help me. And *you're* the one who's impressed by wealth and possessions. That's why you've been so afraid you might never write another best seller. Carlos may be rich, he may be obsessed by the de Alvarez tradition, but if I *do* decide to marry him, it will be because *I love him* and for no other reason!'

The betraying words out, Pippa suddenly recalled the silent onlooker, and flushed scarlet, not daring to look at him.

'Pippa, *tu queria.*' Two warm strong hands came down upon her shoulders, turning her towards him, and a finger lifted her chin, so that she must, perforce, meet the burning, questioning intensity of blue eyes.

As she swayed involuntarily towards him, enfolded, moulded to the lean length of him, Pippa was totally oblivious to Monty's outraged, disgusted snort of defeat.

Pippa wished afterwards she could have remembered in more detail the events of her wedding day. But the brief hours before the hastily arranged and necessarily quiet service—because of the period of mourning for Felipe—passed in a haze of unreality. It was as though Carlos having heard her admission of love, having made her repeat it, demonstrate it most satisfactorily, was afraid she would again retract it.

She'd tried, once or twice, in those busy days before the wedding, to speak to him of the past.

'I want to tell you, Carlos, about—about that time— six years ago—about Peter and ...'

'No!' Firmly he had grasped her arms, his eyes and face forbidding. 'Your past is yours we have agreed—as *my* past is my own. Since—since Carmela died, there have been women—I could not live like a monk—but I do not intend to tell you of them—and you will please not speak to me of ...'

'But Carlos, there's something you ought to ...'

'No! I forbid it!' And he had walked away from her.

Because of his adamant refusal to discuss their earlier lives—his and hers, before they had met—Pippa hesitated to question him on the subject of children. Even though she loved him, a certain delicacy of mind forbade that she raise a subject so personal to him when he had not, and though her own knowledge of his undisclosed secret still nagged at her, she consoled herself with the fact that, later, when they were—more intimate—she quivered at the thought—*then* he would tell her and she would be able to reassure him that *he* was the only important thing in her life—he and his love.

An issue they *had* discussed was that of advising James Lang of their impending marriage.

'We could telephone your father,' Carlos had said. 'but it is very short notice. Would he be able to come? *Would* he come?'

'I don't know,' Pippa confessed. 'I—I think I'd rather tell him myself, face to face, than over the phone. Could—could we go to England—after——' she flushed, 'after our h-honeymoon? Then, when he sees how—how happy we are, he won't mind so much, perhaps . . .'

'You are very protective of your father's feelings.' Carlos did not sound as though he found this a fault in her and Pippa took courage from the fact.

'Yes. I know you and he haven't seen eye to eye when you've met—but I'm sure, when he knows you better—knows that I—I . . .' Again the flush and this time there was no need to complete her sentence, since Carlos found other occupation for her lips.

Luisa and Inez, both in deepest black, were their only witnesses at the little blue-tiled village church, where only the previous day, Felipe had been interred. Monty, in high dudgeon, had taken himself off bag and baggage to a hotel in Lisbon, where he was waiting for Peter to come and escort him home.

Pippa was glad to see—perhaps her only coherent thought of the day—the new, though still tentative, *rapprochement* between her mother and Luisa. It was as though, with Felipe's death, her mother's passionate wildness had died, too. She was quiet, dignified in her grief, making her a more likeable person, so that it was possible after all to see how the devout Mariana might be her daughter.

Carlos had told Pippa that he wouldn't be at all surprised to see Inez and Luisa make a permanent home together, with their memories of their shared youth, memories of Felipe. To Pippa this seemed a little morbid, but if it would in any way console the two women for their mutual loss . . .

With no time for many arrangements to be made, Carlos had decreed with no demur from a still bemused Pippa that they would spend their honeymoon in Lisbon.

When the apartment in Lisbon had been mentioned,

Pippa had pictured a modern purpose-built block—not a very romantic setting for a honeymoon, she thought wistfully, as, Carlos driving, they approached the outskirts of the city. But did it really matter? she wondered, with a shy sideways glance at the profile of her husband. It was people that mattered, not places. Surely the most prosaic of backgrounds could become beautiful seen through the eyes of love?

But she was in for a pleasant surprise. The de Alvarez apartment was in the Old Town, in the best known, the most ancient quarter—the Alfama. Above the Alfama, in the Portas do Sol, stood the fine old houses of the rich and it was in one of these, beautifully restored, that Pippa found herself alone with her new husband.

Until this moment everything had happened so fast that there had been little time for reflection or for nerves. Now at last, the reality of her situation struck home and she stared about her exotic but unfamiliar surroundings with dazed fear-dilated eyes.

'The view is worth seeing, Pippa,' Carlos suggested, his voice blessedly matter-of-fact. She had known how to deal with Carlos the stranger, Carlos the apparently hostile cousin, but Carlos the lover, the husband? Any postponement of that problem was suddenly welcome.

The vine-shaded balcony to which he led her did indeed offer an admirable view—of rooftops aflutter with pigeons, and of the River Tagus, busy with ocean liners and smaller boats. As they stood, his arm around her shoulders, from the slopes below them arose the friendly murmur of city life.

'It—it's beautiful,' she murmured, still painfully shy of him.

'And so are you, Pippa.' He had not been looking out over the city at all, but down into her face, slightly pale with the apprehension she felt.

'Me? Beautiful?' She made a little sound of incredulity.

'But of course—and soon you will be even more beautiful,' his voice became husky and his words increased her anxious pulse beat, 'but you must be tired. These have been very eventful days. Why not bathe and change? I will do the same. By that time a meal will have been prepared for us.' He moved around opening doors. 'The bedroom, the bathrooms—yours and mine.'

The bedroom! With nothing to take her mind off the hours ahead, left alone, Pippa began to feel even more afraid.

Inez's wedding present to her had been a full set of luxurious lingerie, a nightdress and matching négligé. Goodness only knew how her mother had found time to purchase so many things in the time available, but Pippa was grateful to her. Her own wardrobe was woefully inadequate for the wife of Carlos de Alvarez.

She wished, however, as she inspected the nightdress, that she could have had some say in its choice. She would never have selected anything half as revealing as the sinuous fall of soft silk, which, if anything, showed off rather than concealed the full curves of her breasts, the tapering line of waist, the swell of hips. Even with the négligé over it, it was almost indecent, she thought worriedly.

By the time she emerged into the sitting-room feeling painfully self-conscious, a trolley had been wheeled in, bearing a meal that looked far too substantial for someone in her nervous condition to tackle.

She started uncontrollably as the door opened and Carlos entered, clad only in a thigh-length silk robe which revealed a long length of leg, surprisingly muscular for someone of his ascetic build—muscular and disturbingly coated with a fine sheen of still damp hair.

'Shall we eat?' His manner was prosaic enough as he poured wine for them both and she nodded, but as she suspected, she could scarcely swallow more than a few mouthfuls. Panic filled her throat. What had she done? How did she come to be here, in this unfamiliar room, with the man who was after all little more than a stranger? And soon he would expect the deepest intimacies of her. Suppose—suppose he were disappointed in her? He was an experienced man. He . . .'

'I think,' Carlos said and now he sounded faintly amused, 'that it would be as well if we dispensed with the food—for the moment. You will enjoy it far more— afterwards.' He rose from his chair and came towards her, holding out a hand. 'Come, Pippa, do not look so much like a lamb being led to the slaughter.'

She did not take the hand, but stared up at him, grey eyes wide, stricken.

'N-not yet. I-I think I should like s-some more wine.'

'Dutch courage?' he enquired, his thumb circling the palm of the soft hand he held. 'That will not be necessary. Come,' he repeated.

She swallowed drily as she rose and allowed herself to be led into the bedroom—towards the bed.

'I—I've just realised—I—I hardly know you,' she whispered pleadingly, as firmly he pushed her down on to the side of the bed, sat beside her. 'And,' desperately, 'you hardly know anything about me really. Carlos, I know you forbade me to—to—but I must tell you *now*. I . . .'

'Very soon you will know everything there is to know,' he murmured huskily, and as she blushed deep crimson, 'as I will know everything about you.' His mouth possessed hers and once again her opportunity to tell the truth about the past was lost.

Warm caresses, kisses, at once tender and dominating, soothed her fears until she rested quiescently, submissively against him. Slowly he removed the nightdress and négligé. They had served little purpose after all, she thought dazedly, except to inflame his desire.

Just how many women had he made love to? she wondered, as lips and fingers that spoke of undoubted experience explored her trembling body, made him the master of her secrets, while the musky scents of him assailed her nostrils. But he was right—it didn't matter if there had been others, she realised, that was in the past. Now was hers. Theirs.

'Why are you so afraid?' he whispered softly against her ear. 'This it not the first time for you. Ah,' as she stiffened, but before she could answer, 'perhaps *that* is what troubles you? That you are no virgin? It need not, *amada*.' His voice was tender. 'We are agreed, are we not? You were young, a little reckless. But now there is no need for shame, no longer any need to keep hidden the existence of the child. We shall take him into our home, although there can be no question of his . . .'

'No, Carlos!'

Pippa went rigid. Oh, no! He still thought . . . Oh, how blind she'd been, how stupidly romantically blind. It hadn't been love after all that had made him so urgent to marry her. Why had she allowed her pride to get her into this mess? If she'd told him right away at the start of their acquaintance that there was no child, that would have been the end of it. There would have been no point in his pursuing her, making her fall in love with him against her will.

Frenziedly, she began to struggle.

'No, Carlos, no. You don't understand. I . . .'

'I understand you very well, my Pippa, I think. You ...'

'You *don't* understand,' she cried in anguish. 'Carlos, you must listen to me this time. There *is* no child. There never has been. I was never pregnant. It was a mistake. I wanted to tell you before but you wouldn't listen.'

Shudderingly, she awaited the explosion of wrath, but his voice was gentle, amused even.

'Pippa, there's no need to lie to me—not now ...'

'I'm *not* lying!' She gave a bitter little laugh. 'I'm sorry to disappoint you. It's ironic, isn't it? You married me so you could get your hands on the only remaining de Alvarez blood—my son!' The laughter turned to hysteria, racking her body with sobs, her voice rising high and unnatural. 'Well, there isn't a son. I only *thought* I was pregnant ...'

'Pippa!' He sounded angry now. 'Don't *lie* to me.'

'I know why you don't want to believe me,' she screamed the words at him. 'Because you can't have children. You're ...'

Her words, words which in her right mind she would never have been callous enough to taunt him with, were cut off, as, ruthlessly cruel, his mouth crushed her lips, his weight crushed the breath from her body.

'Yes, damn you!' he said between those savage, hurtful kisses. 'I'm *infertile*. That was what you were going to say?'

'Yes!' she sobbed. 'Yes. Did you think I'd never find out? Weren't you ever going to tell me?'

He lifted himself so that he could look down into her drowned, accusing eyes. He spoke more soberly.

'I didn't think it was necessary. Luisa told me that you knew—and yet you agreed to marry me—and since, as I believed, you had a child already, I didn't think it would matter to you so much. I thought your maternal instincts would already have been satisfied. But now,' his tone was savage once more, 'I may not be able to father a son, Pippa, but I am still a man, still capable of . . .'

'No!' She saw his face convulse anew with anger, knew what he intended, but he was too strong for her. 'No, Carlos, no!'

Her struggles became weaker, the angry tears futile sobs of rage and despair, her body one aching need for physical release.

Tears trickled from her eyes, her blood pounded in her ears and she moaned her defeat as, treacherously, her body gave way to the pulsating desire he was evoking and she felt herself move sensually, wantonly against him.

Their mutual anger was an added stimulant to sensation, as they sought fiercely to wound each other with their caresses, his fingers hard and probing, her nails lacerating his naked back.

Then, she cried out against the painful thrust of him—a pain that lasted only for a second, as he swept her on and upward with him into a shattering, bitter-sweet ecstasy.

The moment passed. There was no languorous aftermath, as he flung her from him, limp, passion spent, yet sick at heart. Listlessly, she gazed up at him out of tear-drenched eyes, as he stood over the bed, chest still heaving, his swarthy skin flushed, bedewed with perspiration.

'Damn you!' he whispered. 'Damn you!'

CHAPTER NINE

PIPPA woke to an aching head, an aching body, but worst of all to an aching heart.

Beside her the bed was empty—as it had been all night. His indictment hurled at her, Carlos had stalked out into the night.

A trembling hand to her painful brow, she sat on the side of the bed, trying to summon up enough strength for the few paces that would take her to the bathroom. Oh God, what was she going to do? Was there ever such a coil? Right from the start her instincts, her better judgement, had warned her against involvement with Carlos de Alvarez. Yet somewhere along the way, the fine edge of those instincts had become blurred, her judgement overthrown. She had been duped into thinking that, all other motives apparently disposed of, he wanted to marry her for herself.

Well, his deceit had received the reward it merited, she brooded, as she automatically showered and dried, dressed and tried with make-up to disguise the worst of last night's ravages to her face—she had cried herself to sleep.

Yes, it served him right—there was no child he might claim as having even a drop of de Alvarez blood. But if it served him right, why was her foolish heart still inclined to mourn over the bitter disappointment he must feel?

Despite the shower, her attempts to restore her appearance, Pippa had never felt as dreadful as she did right now—not only physically but also mentally. Where had Carlos gone last night? she agonised. When would he return? *Would* he return? How was she to face him?

She couldn't! Suddenly she knew quite inarguably that she couldn't bear to face him—any more than he would want to see the woman who couldn't give him what he wanted. He must think she'd been deliberately lying to him all those weeks—lying by implication, when she'd refused to discuss the whereabouts, the existence of a child.

In a sudden frenzy of activity, Pippa began to pack— just the barest essentials. She couldn't stay here. She had to get away before Carlos came back as he obviously must some time.

As she hurled things into a suitcase, her senses were acutely alert for any sound that might herald his return, afraid now that he might walk in before she could make good her escape.

Her passport? Yes, she had it. Thank goodness, she still had her traveller's cheques. There had been no occasion to spend any money while she'd been at the Quinta.

Throughout the taxi ride to the airport she looked constantly over her shoulder, half expecting to be pursued. But why should Carlos put himself to the trouble, even when he did discover she'd gone? She no longer had anything he wanted.

Due to a cancellation, there was a seat available on the next flight out and only half an hour to wait—a half-hour which, in her nervous state, seemed endless.

Crowds of people thronged the departure lounge and a dismayed Pippa recognised two of her fellow travellers—Monty and Peter. What rotten luck that her ignominious escape should coincide with their journey!

She managed to remain unobserved until their flight was called, then, crossing the tarmac, almost inevitably Peter spotted her. On his own, she was sure Monty would have ignored her. She had burned all her boats where he was concerned. But Peter, though he must be aware of Monty's displeasure with her, was all smiles.

'Decided England's best after all, Pippa?' He flung a free arm across her shoulders and dropped a clumsy kiss somewhere near her hairline. 'Good for you. You don't want to go and marry a foreigner.' Then, to her further dismay, 'We must try and sit together.'

Fortunately that wasn't possible, for Pippa much preferred to be alone with her thoughts, however unpleasant. She had no desire for Monty's shrewd eyes to be witness to her unhappiness. He would be maliciously triumphant. As it was, he must be curious as to the reasons for her presence on this flight—alone.

Take-off accomplished and pursuit now impossible, was it relief she felt, or an added grief? Hadn't she half hoped Carlos would *want* to prevent her leaving? But perhaps he still didn't know she'd left. *Would* he follow her when he found out?

Instead of such vain reflections, Pippa tried to concentrate her mind on future plans. Home first—to Little Pennyfeather—her father. That could involve some very awkward explanations, unless . . .? Her gaze fell speculatively on the wide gold band that had been on her finger for so short a while. Unless she removed her ring? In the euphoria of her forthcoming marriage, she had looked forward to telling her father face to face of her love and happiness, confident that she could make him understand and accept, but now James need never know what a fool she'd been—a disloyal fool, moreover.

Reluctantly, tears pricking her eyes, she slid the ring from her finger and placed it in her purse. It left no mark, no sign at all now that she had ever been married.

At Heathrow, Peter insisted that Pippa shared their car for the drive into Suffolk, placing her in the front seat beside him. Pippa could feel Monty's silent displeasure; he spoke not a word for the whole journey.

'Here we are—safe and sound. How's that for service?' Peter braked showily on the gravel drive outside James Lang's front door. 'I'm staying over for a few days,' he told Pippa as he carried her suitcase, 'so we'll be able to see something of each other.'

Pippa, tired, travel weary, dreading the forthcoming encounter—how could she hide her unhappiness from her father?—hadn't the strength to argue. She made a non-committal sound and pushed open the huge front door that was rarely locked by day. She was home.

It *was* her home—but it could never be the same as before—not now she'd had a glimpse of a very different kind of home, the kind that offered a husband, happiness, physical fulfilment. By comparison this was a barren place. But she must put a good face on it, to meet her father.

'It's good to have you back, Pippa, love,' James Lang said as Pippa hugged him. 'No—no problems with the de Alvarez family?' He didn't ask after Inez by name, but that was understandable. 'Short trip, wasn't it? Thought Mortimer wanted to travel?'

'That's what I thought, too. Dad,' abruptly, 'I'm not working for Monty any more. We—we had a disagreement and—well—I want to try my hand at writing my own stuff. I'll get a part-time job—I wouldn't expect you to support me ...'

'There's no need for that. I ...'

'Honestly, Dad, I'd rather be independent. I think I can write but it will take time—and then I've to convince a publisher ...'

'All right—and I may be able to help you. Never did care much for you working up at that chap's house—odd bird. Leave it to me. I'll have a word with Rosemary.' Rosemary was a teacher at Pippa's former school and she knew her father saw the other woman from time to time. 'She said they were needing a part-time secretary. Just up your street, I should think, eh?'

The job wasn't a particularly stimulating one, but it *was* a job and at least it meant an early start each morning, with little time for brooding. In the afternoon, Pippa shut herself away in her bedroom and typed, but with a very different subject matter. She had always had an outstanding ability with words, but now her own heightened emotions seemed to add a strength and a depth that had been lacking before.

The story of Pedro the First and Inez needed more research of course, entailing trips to public libraries, but the basic details were there, in her head. Interrelated with their tragic story, she wove another romance, fictional, but of equally passionate intensity, not realising that she gave to her characters the aspect, traits and motives that formed so great a part of herself—and of Carlos de Alvarez.

'You look a bit peaky,' was her father's perceptive remark over breakfast six or seven weeks after her return home. 'Overdoing things a bit, aren't you?—working at the school every morning and then typing away upstairs till God knows what hour of the night? You don't eat enough to keep a hen alive either,' he observed, watching her pick listlessly at a fried breakfast that normally she would have demolished with good appetite.

She had been off her food the last week or two, but that was a natural outcome of the unhappiness that seemed constantly to fill her throat, threatening to choke her. What little she did eat had to be forced down. But now, as her father pressed another rasher of bacon upon her, suggested a fried egg, she felt her stomach revolt. Hastily she rose from the table, ran from the room, gaining the bathroom only just in time, as wave after wave of nausea racked her. She must be sickening for something. Even her unhappiness, the longing for Carlos, the constant wondering why he had made no effort to contact her, couldn't make her feel this ghastly, she decided.

The spasm over, she went to work as usual, making a mental note to visit the doctor if the symptoms recurred, which they did for the next two mornings, persisting sometimes throughout the day, making her drawn of face and listless.

Old Mac the family doctor had known Pippa since birth. He had delivered her, and now he seemed to be observing her in a very curious, almost awkward manner. He cleared his throat two or three times, then began, 'Has it struck you, girlie, that you might be— might be—pregnant?'

Pippa shook her head.

'Impossible,' she said flatly.

'So I would have thought. You're not married, but

these days, ah, well—and all the symptoms. Let's just have a wee look at you, girlie, shall we?'

Ten minutes later, a very shaken Pippa emerged from the surgery, a prescription in her hand and the staggering knowledge that she was indeed pregnant. Yet how could she be? Carlos had made love to her once—if that angry, punishing possession could be called love—and besides, he couldn't ... Luisa had said. And he hadn't denied it, when she'd thrown those hurtful words at him.

But even larger than this insoluble problem loomed that of what she was to do now. Doctor Mac had assumed she was unmarried and she hadn't enlightened him, but it wouldn't be long before her condition was evident to everyone—so what did she tell her father? And—did she tell Carlos?

Her father would have to be told the truth, she concluded finally, after hours of anguished deliberation. The knowledge of her marriage to Carlos, that she had kept it a secret, would hurt him, but she couldn't let him come to the same conclusion as the doctor, that her child was the result of a careless affair—not after that other incident six years ago.

It never occurred to her to do anything other than have her baby. Any other course of action would have been totally repugnant to her. It did occur to her—and she could not put the thought from her—to wonder what Carlos would feel, if he knew that she carried his child. But it didn't take much deliberation to find the answer. He'd be there like a shot, insisting that she return to Portugal with him, that his child be brought up at the Quinta de Estrella. Or—she felt quite faint at the thought—he might want to take the child, but not

her. Could he do that? Claim his child? Take it away
from her?

Her first reaction was that Carlos must never know,
that this child would be hers. After all, she argued with
her conscience, he had no reason for even believing it
existed and what he didn't know couldn't harm him.

But that wasn't true. Whether he knew or not she *was*
harming him, if she kept from him the one thing he
wanted most in life—a son—for somehow she had no
doubt at all that it would be a boy, the heir to the de
Alvarez fortune and traditions. If you really loved him,
she told herself, you'd tell him. But then she *did* love
him, so much so that she wanted his love for herself, not
for the fruits of her body alone.

Another alternative—one that made her shudder, but
must be considered—was that she should write and offer
him his freedom. After all, there had been another
woman to whom he'd contemplated marriage. If he had
given Pippa a child, why shouldn't he be as successful
with this other woman, whoever she was? Then she
remembered, Carlos was a Catholic—for him divorce
would be unthinkable. But that wasn't *her* fault!

So her thoughts swung backwards and forwards in the
weeks that followed, until at last conscience could no
longer be ignored. Whatever the consequences to
herself, Carlos had the right to know.

It took a long time and several sheets of crumpled
notepaper before she was satisfied with her letter, and in
the end it was a formal, stilted effort, relating only the
facts, revealing nothing of her own pain, her longing.
And then she waited—waited in vain. There was no
reply, not even an acknowledgement that her letter had
been received. Had it gone astray?

She wrote again—and this time, within days, there was a reaction—her letter was returned, unopened, and there was no doubt that the covering envelope was addressed in Carlos's strong bold handwriting. He had rejected the overture that had cost her so much humbled pride and pain. For a few days this indignation heated her blood, but it was not long before she realised with a chilling certainty that her duty was not yet fulfilled. It behoved her to try again. This time she would telephone, and if Carlos himself took the call, she would blurt out the information before he could hang up on her.

The clarity of the line was unbelievable—it was difficult to imagine the miles of earth and sea that lay between her Suffolk home and the Quinta de Estrella, but it was a servant's voice that answered—she should have considered that possibility—first in Portuguese and then, as Pippa spoke, in halting English.

Long after she had replaced the receiver, Pippa sat staring at the instrument in anguished disbelief. The servant had recognised her voice and firmly but politely had made it understood that the Senhor refused to take any telephone calls from England—and no, he regretted he was not even permitted to accept messages from the Senhora.

Well, she'd tried, Pippa fumed, she *had* tried—now it was Carlos's own fault if he never learnt of the existence of his child. But even anger could not ease her aching heart.

After the first shock, the reaction of hurt anger, James Lang had been brusquely kind to his daughter. The child, after all, he told Pippa, would be *his* grandchild. Pippa had, he contended, done more than enough to appease her conscience where Carlos was concerned. Her marriage should remain a secret, known only to the two of them, the father's identity concealed.

'But you must have been mad to have anything to do with that fellow,' he concluded, 'I know women are supposed to find foreigners attractive, but you can't successfully mix two cultures. Believe me, I know!'

And for the time being at least, Pippa left her father in that belief. He would find it utterly inexplicable that in spite of what she knew of her own mother, she should actually have fallen in love with a de Alvarez, that, in spite of everything, she still loved Carlos. And it would be far too painful an experience to have to relate all the details of her stay in Portugal, its conclusion, its knife-sharp finale.

Another factor in James's acceptance was his increasing personal happiness. His friendship with Rosemary Leigh was growing deeper and finally he had decided to put in motion an application for a divorce.

'You won't mind?' he asked Pippa diffidently. 'If I get married again?'

'Not a bit.' Pippa was quite sincere in her good wishes. 'Why shouldn't you be happy? While I was in Portugal,' she hesitated a little, this was the first reference she had made to her mother since her return, 'I got to understand *Mãe* a lot better. But—if she weren't my mother—I don't think I'd like her very much. She—she hasn't really grown up. In spite of being married and having me and Mariana, she's still the wilful girl who was determined to pursue a married man and defied her father. I like Rosemary,' she went on, 'and as soon as I can, I'll find somewhere else to live. You won't want me around.'

But on the contrary, both James and Rosemary seemed very anxious that Pippa should stay at the farmhouse. Both were too old to start a family, but insisted that they relished the idea of having a baby in the house. Their kindness to her during her seemingly endless pregnancy often made an emotion difficult to bear well up inside her lonely heart.

It was at times like these that she thanked God for her ability to write, to pour out her feelings on paper. She knew it was difficult to judge one's own work, but she really felt that what she was writing was good. She only hoped some publisher would think the same.

Carlos's rejection of her letters and her telephone call hurt, dreadfully. There had been no word from him, not even to learn if she'd arrived home safely. But that merely demonstrated the depth of his feeling for her—or rather the lack of it.

Peter had been attentive during the few days he'd stayed with Monty, but once he'd returned to London, his letters and telephone calls had tailed off; he was discouraged perhaps by Pippa's lack-lustre response, and she was glad of it. She didn't want Peter to know she was pregnant. From Monty he would have learned of her brief involvement with Carlos and would very speedily put two and two together. The fewer people who knew of her child's parentage the better. There was little danger of her encountering Monty himself. He had retreated into reclusiveness again and was, presumably, working on his novel. Pippa had to admit to a little curiosity as to how it would succeed without her help.

'It's a girl—a lovely little girl.' The midwife's voice impinged upon Pippa's consciousness.

It had not been an easy birth and she was still in a drug-induced haze.

'A girl?' For a moment she was dismayed. She had been so confident that it would be a boy, a boy who would grow up to look like his father. But then a shaft of triumph went through her. A boy was what Carlos would have wanted. This little girl would be hers—all hers—and she need not feel so guilty about keeping the child's existence a secret from her father. Even so, 'I shall call her Carla,' she decided.

When Carla was almost a year old, so like her father that a pang smote Pippa every time she looked at the child, three events occurred. James Lang obtained his final decree and married Rosemary Leigh, Monty's book was published, and so was Pippa's.

'An amazing first work by a promising new novelist,' the critics said of it. 'An historical writer in all the best traditions of English literature. We look forward to Miss Lang's next book.'

Monty's book received mixed reviews, favourable on the whole, but it was obvious to everyone that the maestro's light was dimming.

On an impulse which she immediately regretted, Pippa sent Luisa a copy of her book. She often thought about the older woman, wondering if she had come to terms at all with the loss of her brother, whether or not she and Inez had set up house together.

But why had she sent Luisa the book? In the aftermath of regret she examined her motives. Hadn't there been some underlying hope that Carlos would get to know about it—see that she had made the grade as a writer, in spite of all his prognostications to the contrary?

A week or so later, she received a short letter of acknowledgement, but that was all it was. It enclosed good wishes and congratulations from Inez on her success, but there was no mention of anyone else—of the person about whom she still wished to know in spite of everything.

Suffolk. Little Pennyfeather. For only the third time in his life, Carlos was making this journey, but a journey he had never expected to make again. Why then *was* he making his way once more over the familiar route, over the river bridge, past the little grey church? He knew— but had that knowledge come too late?

The first time he'd come this way, it had been with a sense of reluctant duty, a promise he'd made to Inez, that he would visit her daughter, try and persuade her to see her mother. But then he had not known the depths of Inez's guile.

He'd never had any wish to marry his cousin Inez. At thirteen no thoughts of marriage had even entered his head. And she was so much older than he, scornful of the young orphaned relative who'd lived since the age of three under her father's roof. Probably she resented him too, for she must know he would one day inherit the Quinta de Estrella.

So he'd been relieved rather than piqued when his cousin had run off with the young Englishman. But then the promise had been demanded of him. If his cousin Inez should have a daughter of her marriage, he must seek her out and marry her instead. The de Alvarez blood must remain as undiluted as possible. The solemnity of his promise had been emphasised by the placing of his young hand upon the family Bible.

Had it never occurred to his uncle de Alvarez that an English granddaughter might not be willing to have her future thus decided for her? Carlos doubted it. A fanatic where family tradition was concerned, a despot in his own home, it had probably never crossed his uncle's mind that elsewhere families existed more democratically.

As Carlos grew up, the promise had almost faded from his mind, absorbed as he was with his friends, his career, and, inevitably, a succession of attractive young women, each one hoping to become the future Senhora de Alvarez. But Carlos had been seriously drawn to none of them, until he'd met Carmela Monteiro, the much younger sister of Felipe and Luisa, and had fallen in love with her, and not even the anger of his uncle—his warning that the breaking of a solemn vow would have its own retribution—had dissuaded him from marrying her.

Carlos was a religious man, but not to the point of superstition and he had always firmly refused to consider his childless union or the loss of his wife as divine punishment.

Shortly after Carmela's death with other members of her family, Inez had unexpectedly arrived in Portugal with her obsessive determination to remain within visiting distance of the now bereaved Felipe Monteiro. Reluctantly, Carlos had offered her the protection of his home, but he had attached absolutely no conditions, other than that she behave circumspectly and this— though thanks only to Luisa and to Felipe himself—she had done. But he knew now that she *had* lied—for her own ends—to her daughter. A meeker, penitent Inez had admitted it.

The hired car slowed a little as Carlos negotiated the

turn into the farmyard. Would he find Pippa here? How would she receive him? *Would* she receive him, or would he find himself turned from the door by a testy father, as on that first occasion six years ago?

After so many years at the Quinta, when, at last, Carlos had hinted delicately that it might be an idea for her to find her own house, take a female companion— mentioned to her that he was seriously considering remarrying—only then, he now realised, had Inez even recalled the existence of her elder daughter and begged him to visit Little Pennyfeather during one of his business trips, to bring her news of Pippa. With apparent wistfulness, she'd told him, 'Philippa, my elder daughter, must be sixteen now—almost old enough to marry. Then I suppose I shall never see her again.'

Carlos had had absolutely no intention of marrying his young cousin. His desire to remarry at all was merely for reasons of convenience, since he knew it to be unlikely that he would ever sire a de Alvarez heir.

But he'd had to go to England on business for the wine exporters he represented and, if only for the sake of peace under his roof, he had agreed to take Inez's messages to her daughter, ineffectually the first time— but on the second occasion . . . And he had not, after all, remarried, because . . .

'Good God! You've got a nerve! What the hell do you think you're doing here?' Thus James Lang, as he opened his front door, spoke to the man who was now his son-in-law.

'I've come to see Pippa!'

'Have you indeed? Well, I doubt if *she'll* want to see *you*.'

'Perhaps you would ask *her*?' Carlos suggested with determined courtesy.

Muttering, James Lang departed, and, left in the large drawing-room which he remembered from his last visit, Carlos looked around him with sudden interest. There had been changes made here. It was summer, of course, and therefore no fire burnt in the grate, but the room had been redecorated and there was no atmosphere of dampness or of dogs. There were distinct feminine touches. Had Pippa wrought these changes?

On his first visit to Little Pennyfeather he hadn't even been allowed to cross the threshold of the house, and he'd felt a sense of righteous indignation as he strode along the riverbank. After all his trouble, going out of his way on Inez's behalf, he had been turned from James Lang's door like an unwelcome tradesman. Then had come the incident of dragging what he'd thought to be a half drowned child from the water.

As vividly as though it were yesterday, he could remember the first glimpse he'd had of that child's face—the child-woman, as he'd thought of her from then on. The distinctive features of her face had remained with him down the years, haunted him, so that countless times, he'd scoffed at himself—a man of thirty-four as he'd been then, scion of a noble family, unable to put from his mind the wistful promise of beauty shown by a sixteen-year-old girl who, by her own admission, was no better than she ought to be.

His second visit, almost two years ago now, had been made even more reluctantly. He had made it crystal clear to Inez by now that he did not intend to marry, but he had agreed to her piteous plea that at least Pippa might be invited to visit her. Devious Inez!

Seeing the girl again, realising that his child-woman and Inez's daughter were one and the same, had come as quite a shock to Carlos, as had the sudden surge of feeling he'd experienced—sensations that had filled him with contrary emotions.

Pippa's first reaction to the news of Carlos's arrival was to refuse to see him. But she was no longer a child, whose father could fend off unwelcome visitors for her. Besides, her heart, always a traitor to common sense, longed for just one more sight of him, and curiosity, her besetting sin, made her wonder just why he had come— after all this time.

He looked taller than ever in the low-beamed drawing-room. His back was turned towards her and he had not heard her enter. For a moment or two, Pippa was able to feast her hungry eyes unobserved. Tall, as lean and muscular as ever—or was he perhaps a little more gaunt that the last time she'd seen him? His hair perhaps a little more liberally sprinkled with grey? Then he turned and the familiar piercing glance of azure blue eyes seemed with their intensity to sear her face and form, his raw vibrant masculinity filling the room with its aura, making its generous proportions actually claustrophobic. She fought for breath.

'Pippa!' He made a slight move towards her, but she made a little sound of protest and he stopped.

'Why are you here, Carlos?' she asked, forcing herself to speak quietly, calmly. There seemed no reason why he should have come now.

'I wanted to see you again,' he said huskily.

'After all this time?' She was coldly incredulous,

though her knees trembled and her heart seemed to ricochet from rib to rib.

'I didn't come before, because . . .'

Damn it! She wasn't giving him any help at all, just standing there, staring at him with those great grey eyes of hers. They seemed even more enormous than he remembered, or was that just because her face was more fine-drawn, giving it an added maturity, an ethereal quality she had lacked before?

He'd guessed immediately on his return to the apartment what Pippa had done. The untidy heap of abandoned clothes, the absence of her suitcase had told their story. He'd guessed at the airport and he'd guessed right. But he'd arrived too late—or just in time—to see her crossing the tarmac with young Makin's arm around her. *Deus*, he'd thought, she hadn't wasted much time in contacting her former lover. Furious pride had made him destroy her first letter unread, return the second also unopened, and he had not trusted himself to hear her voice.

'I didn't come because I thought you would not want to see me.'

'What changed your mind? Or made you think I might have changed mine?'

'Two things—the book you sent Luisa. It could have been a message that you hadn't forgotten Portugal, that you hadn't forgotten me—you used the story I gave you—your hero and heroine—they resembled us so closely—you and I.'

'An author is a fool if she doesn't use whatever sources are available to her.' Pippa would not admit to any such sentimentality.

'I cannot, I will not, believe that *you* wrote that book

in any such mood of cynicism. I have never forgotten your words to Senhor Mortimer when ...'

Pippa flushed. She'd said rather a lot to Monty that day, including the fact that she would marry Carlos for love and no other reason.

'You said there were two things,' she reminded him, banishing the dangerous memory.

'I was in London last week. I met Senhor Makin and he said he had not seen you for nearly two years. That seemed to me to be strange, since I had seen you leave Portugal with him.'

He'd *seen* her leave. Then he *had* come to the airport! Again Pippa's heart leapt erratically, but she showed no emotion.

'Pippa! *Have* you forgotten about me, these last two years?'

'It's not exactly easy,' she said sarcastically, 'to forget you're married, not free to ...'

'Not free?' he said sharply. 'Have you wished to be free?'

But the answer to that was something else Pippa was not prepared to admit. Besides, she was in an agony of apprehension, lest Rosemary and Carla come back from their afternoon walk. If Carlos once saw the child, he could not fail to recognise her heredity, and she could not predict his reaction.

'Could we come to the point?' she said, deliberately brusque. 'I've interrupted my work to see you ...'

'Ah yes—your work—the successful author! Are you writing another book, Pippa? Is it to be as successful as the first?'

Was it? She doubted it. That first book had been written out of a welter of emotion that time had dulled a little. If she were ever to write anything remotely as good, those emotions would need to be honed razor-sharp again—and there was only one person who could evoke those emotions in her . . .

'Never mind my work. What do you *want*, Carlos?'

'You!' he said simply. And in one fluid movement he was at her side.

'Carlos!' She said his name warningly. She was very close to tears, but he mustn't know that.

'I mean it, Pippa. I tried—God knows I tried—but I haven't been able to get you out of my mind.' His hand went up to her hair, restrained as always nowadays in its severe chignon. 'Why do you wear your hair like this?' he demanded. 'You should wear it so!' The pins cascaded to the floor and his fingers plunged into the red-gold luxuriance.

'No, Carlos, please . . .' She felt the old familiar trembling begin as his hands moved from her hair to her neck and now to the full swell of her breasts. As his hands grasped her waist, she cried out in agonised protest, recognising that her desire for him, so rigidly suppressed these past two years, lay dangerously close to the surface. 'Let me go,' she moaned, but her words were ignored, any repetition prevented by the pressure of his mouth on hers.

He was holding her so closely now that she could scarcely breathe, his hands moving over her in a series of fierce caresses, sensually erotic. She tried to fight the passion that was ensnaring her senses, but she was helpless, dizzy, clutching at his shoulders for the support she needed.

'I am never going to let you go again, Pippa,' he stated raggedly.

'D-don't you think I m-might have something to say about that?' she demanded, angry with her voice for sounding so tremulously husky, so revealingly aroused.

'All I want to hear you say is what you said once before—and only once, more is the pity. You said two years ago that you loved me.'

'B-but I d-d ...'

'Don't deny it, Pippa.' His voice was stern. 'Don't desecrate something so precious. You said the words, your body reinforced their meaning—you married me, because you *loved me*.'

'Yes!' Her control snapped. The tears fell. 'All right! Maybe I did. But I was a fool ever to fall in love with you.' She wrenched free of him and moved away to lean against the window, her heated face pressed to its cooling glass. 'I don't even know if it *was* love,' she lied desperately. 'Maybe it was only ever phy-physical. Whatever it was, I regretted it almost immediately.'

'Almost?' he murmured.

'When I found out why you'd married me.' She faced him, face tear-wet but defiant.

'And why was that?' The room was between them, but the movement of his eyes over her face and body was as evocative as his caresses had been.

Pippa's body throbbed achingly, needing the sexual satisfaction only he could give her and she hated her body for making it so hard for her to utter the words.

'Because you thought I had a child—because you thought, in default of an heir of your own, he would do—because he bore my blood ...'

'No!' It was an imperious sound, and if she had not been so sure of her facts, Pippa might have been convinced by the angry denial it conveyed. 'No, Pippa, that is *not why* I married you.'

'Don't make it worse, don't lie to me.' Her voice trembled. All she wanted to do was to run into his arms, to be held as only he could hold her; she craved the feel of his body hard against hers. She fought the insidious longing.

'I am not lying to you, Pippa. I have never lied to you. But I have tried to tell you things—*many* things— including the fact that—your flesh and blood or not— Makin's child could never inherit—even though, for your sake, I was prepared to care for him.' Carlos watched the conflicting emotions that ravaged his wife's lovely face, their play his hope of success. 'Do you remember,' he came closer, his voice barely above a whisper, 'the night I rescued you from the river?'

'The night you *thought* you were rescuing me,' she argued faintly. Dispute was the only way she could remain sane in his proximity.

'Shortly after that, I saw your face for the first time. Pippa, your face haunted me—for six long years. I kept telling myself it was ridiculous, that you were a child—a child I didn't even know—I was a grown man, that, after Carmela, I didn't want to fall in love again—and yet ...'

She turned her head away, looking blindly out of the window. She had no answer this time. Oh, he could sound so convincing, but ...

'Pippa, when I came over to England again—two years ago—I had already abandoned all ideas of remarrying—and I certainly had no intention of dragging Inez's daughter back to Portugal so that I could marry her—I beg you to believe that.'

She began to tremble, as he slipped a strong arm about

her waist, drew her against the hard line of his hip-bone.

'But when I saw that *you* were Inez's daughter, that you were the girl I had tried so unsuccessfully to forget ...'

Breathlessly, she fought once more against the temptation to turn into his arms, to give into the seduction of his nearness.

'When you saw who I was, you were shocked and disgusted. You ...'

'No!' Again that fierce contradiction. 'I was afraid—afraid and angry ...'

'Angry I can believe, but you, afraid? Never!'

'I was afraid, *amada*, that in my folly I had left it too late. I should have come back to England sooner, in search of you. You might have married the father of your child. You told me you had not, but then you refused, so scornfully, your mother's invitation to come to Portugal—I could scarcely tell you then how much I wanted you to come—for *my* sake.' With one finger, that old familiar gesture, he lifted her chin. 'Believe me, Pippa, I wanted that more than anything else in the world. If you had not come of your own accord, I should have come to England, again and again ...'

An aching sweetness was beginning to pervade her being, but still she could not quite trust him.

'And when I did come—with Monty—you were angry—you—you accused me of all kinds of dreadful things—and then, when I finally believed in you, you were angry again—I thought it was because I didn't have a child for you to ...'

'No, no and no! I was angry because I thought you were still lying to me, because you didn't trust me with the knowledge of your child's existence. Did not trust me to love you in spite of your one indiscretion. Oh, *amada*, if you knew how little that mattered to me, because you were you! The fact that the child did not exist could make no difference to my love for you.' He stopped then, gazing down into her eyes. 'I was angry too,' he said in a low voice, 'with myself, because— because . . .' he cleared his throat, 'I allowed myself to be wounded by your taunts—at my sterility—and I was not tender with you—as I now wish to be. I am sorry, *amada*.'

'No,' Pippa said brokenly. 'It's I who should be sorry. I should never have said what I did. It was only because I was so hurt. And—and I want to believe you now, but . . .' She shivered as she saw the look of exultation her half-admission had brought to his eyes.

'You *do* still care. You have not taught yourself to hate me? Pippa, doesn't the fact that I want you back—as my wife—in every sense of the word, prove that it is you yourself who are important to me?'

'You wouldn't take my phone calls, you returned my letter . . .'

'Because I did not want to know what they said—I believed you had gone back to Makin.'

Still wary, she tested him further.

'And yet we shall never have any children.'

'No,' he admitted sadly, 'but . . .'

'Are you quite certain?'

His face twisted.

'Pippa, *amada*, over the years—I was married for several years—there were no children. And now,' he said simply, 'there is only you. It is God's will for me,' he added sombrely. 'Some would say it was punishment for breaking my vow, or for the de Alvarez pride over the centuries. But I do not believe that. But there will be no children. Does—does that matter so very much to you, *mi amada*?'

'Oh, Carlos!' She could not deny him or herself any longer. On tiptoe she gave him his answer, pressing her mouth against his.

For an instant he was statue-still, then with a low growl that was half-triumph, half-pain, his lips came down on hers, not fiercely as she had expected, but with a gentle, sensual exploration that seemed to draw her up so that she became a very part of him.

'Pippa!' he groaned, his desire rampant, uncontrollable. 'Is there—is there anywhere we can be private? I do not think I can stand ...'

'Upstairs,' she whispered. 'My room.'

He swept her upstairs with effortless ease, making nothing of the stairs.

'Which way?'

In her room, locked in against the world, time seemed suspended, Pippa lost all conception of time and place as he made love to her, as she responded with all the wanton abandon the months of denial had brought to a peak of agonised wanting. All she knew was the weight, the warmth, the scent of him, his urgent need, its imperious demand. The sensations she experienced were piercingly sweet, as he made love to her until his own hunger and thirst were appeased and they lay, arms wound about each other's trembling bodies.

As later, very much later, they descended the stairs, arms still around each other, Pippa recalled that their sense of isolation had been only an illusion. This was her father's house. She could hear voices in the drawing-room—his and Rosemary's—and one other.

On the bottom step of the staircase, she turned to Carlos.

'There—there's something I haven't told you.'

He looked at her tenderly.

'There was only one thing I wanted to hear and that you have told me—most satisfactorily.'

'No, Carlos. There is one other thing. It may come as a shock to you, but oh, darling, your doctors were wrong.' She hesitated to tell him this about the wife he had loved, but, 'It—it must have been Carmela who—who couldn't ... You *are* capable of fathering a child. You *have* fathered a child.'

He sat down abruptly on the stairs.

'Is this some—some trick, Pippa?' There was anguish in his voice. 'For me, it is not a matter for jest.'

'Come and see!' She drew him up, led him into the drawing-room. 'My father you already know, this is his second wife, Rosemary, and this ...' she held out a hand to the lively dark-haired toddler, 'this is your daughter—Carla.'

In an agony of exquisite emotion, she watched his face, saw the proud mouth quiver, the dark eyes glisten as he looked at his daughter, could be in no doubt about her heritage. Then he turned on Pippa, almost savagely, his hand on her arm, as he marched her out of the room and into the garden.

'That child is almost a year old. Why didn't you tell me? Were you ever going to tell me?' His voice choked on the words.

'I did tell you—at least I tried—my letters—my phone call ...'

'But when I arrived here today—why did you not tell me then?'

'Oh, Carlos—don't you see?—not without knowing that you truly loved me for myself. I *had* to know that.'

'And if I had never come to you?'

She gazed up at him helplessly, then, miraculously his face softened. 'If I had not come to you, my Pippa, it would have been my own stupid fault. But I did come, our destiny saw to that. Some day, somehow, however long it took, I must have come to you. Your heart called to mine, your body to mine. Ah, Pippa, how can I ever repay you for all you have given me today?'

'I *could* suggest a way,' she told him demurely, grey eyes only partly veiled as she observed his reaction. 'Carla is getting extremely spoilt. She could do with a brother.'

Harlequin American Romance

Romances that go one step farther...
American Romance

Realistic stories involving people you can relate to and
care about.

Compelling relationships between the mature men and
women of today's world.

Romances that capture the core of genuine emotions
between a man and a woman.

Join us each month for four new titles wherever paperback
books are sold.
Enter the world of American Romance.

Amro-1

Harlequin Superromance

Here are the longer, more involving stories you have been waiting for . . . Superromance.

Modern, believable novels of love, full of the complex joys and heartaches of real people.

Intriguing conflicts based on today's constantly changing life-styles.

Four new titles every month.
Available wherever paperbacks are sold.

SUPER-1

Keepsake

◆ Harlequin Books

You're never too young to enjoy romance. Harlequin for you . . . and Keepsake, young-adult romances destined to win hearts, for your daughter.

Pick one up today and start your daughter on her journey into the wonderful world of romance.

Two new titles to choose from each month.

ADULTB-1

ATTRACTIVE, SPACE SAVING BOOK RACK

Display your most prized novels on this handsome and sturdy book rack. The hand-rubbed walnut finish will blend into your library decor with quiet elegance, providing a practical organizer for your favorite hard-or soft-covered books.

Only $9.95

Approximately 16" x 8" when assembled

Assembles in seconds!

To order, rush your name, address and zip code, along with a check or money order for $10.70* ($9.95 plus 75¢ postage and handling) payable to *Harlequin Reader Service*:

> Harlequin Reader Service
> Book Rack Offer
> 901 Fuhrmann Blvd.
> P.O. Box 1396
> Buffalo, NY 14269-1396

Offer not available in Canada.

BKR-1A

*New York and Iowa residents add appropriate sales tax.

Harlequin Presents

Coming Next Month

1151 ALWAYS LOVE Emma Darcy
After four years of silent waiting, Genevra is about to try to find out why Luke Stanford never returned to her from Australia. Then Christian Nemo comes into her life—a man so like Luke it sends her into an emotional turmoil!

1152 VILLAIN OF THE PIECE Catherine George
It's unfortunate that the only help available to Lucy and her young son is from Joss Woodbridge—the man who had ruined her life once already. However generous, he's the last man she wants to turn to....

1153 AN EXPERT TEACHER Penny Jordan
Her return for her brother's wedding reinforces all Gemma's feelings of being a misfit in her parents' wealthy world. And after seeing the older, sophisticated Luke she'd unwittingly rejected as a teenager, Gemma is faced with a commitment she's not quite sure she can make.

1154 THE LOVING GAMBLE Flora Kidd
Scottish designer Rachel Dow and investment analyst Ross Fraser meet in the United States, have a whirlwind romance and marry. Only back in Scotland does Rachel begin to suspect that Ross's motives aren't as simple as she'd imagined—and his answers to her questions are unconvincing.

1155 A FLOOD OF SWEET FIRE Sandra Marton
Everything's working well, Blair thinks as she flies to Italy pretending to be Meryl Desmond. Her young socialite boss has reasons to avoid the press. But outside Rome airport she suddenly finds herself victim of a kidnap attempt and captive of a mysterious man called Rhys Hunter....

1156 ILLUSION OF PARADISE Joanna Mansell
Jay Challoner never gave interviews, so journalist Charlie resorts to rather devious methods to spend some time with him. Disappointed when he has to rush off to Ecuador, she gets the shock of her life when he agrees to take her with him!

1157 THE BITTER TASTE OF LOVE Lilian Peake
Used to advising other people, when it comes to her own life Jemma finds things aren't so simple. She's swept into a whirlwind marriage and loves her artistic husband. But she doesn't always understand him—or his explanations about Joanna....

1158 HOT PURSUIT Karen van der Zee
Henk Hofstra pursues Natasha with a single-mindedness that makes her question her cynical vow never to get involved with a man again. Does his determination and their shared Dutch background mean she can really trust him?

Available in March wherever paperback books are sold, or through Harlequin Reader Service:

In the U.S.
901 Fuhrmann Blvd.
P.O. Box 1397
Buffalo, N.Y. 14240-1397

In Canada
P.O. Box 603
Fort Erie, Ontario
L2A 5X3